Tangled in Tinsel

by

N. Jade Gray

Tangled in Tinsel

Cover Art by *Debbie Taylor*

The Wild Rose Press, Inc.
PO Box 708
Adams Basin, NY 14410-0708
Visit us at www.thewildrosepress.com

Publishing History
First Champagne Rose Edition, 2020
Trade Paperback ISBN 978-1-5092-3449-3
Digital ISBN 978-1-5092-3450-9

Published in the United States of America

The scent of pine tickled her nose as she stretched to the top and began weaving the tinsel around the tree.

A pair of hands intercepted hers. "Here, hand the strand to me." Ryder relieved her of the garland and worked it back around the tree.

When his fingers brushed her own, she dropped the twine. The decoration hit the ground and rolled a few feet away.

Taggert giggled and chased it down. "I'll get it." He continued to laugh as he raced around the tree with the garland firmly grasped in his hands.

"Wait, Tag." But her warning was called out too late. He'd wound the twine around the tree and caught her and Ryder's legs in the process. She fell against his chest as she lost her footing.

He gripped her upper arms as he steadied her when she teetered on her feet. "Whoa, buddy. I think you need some help." He spoke to Taggert, but his gaze lingered and twinkled as it locked with hers.

A snicker echoed from the direction of the couch. She could swear she overheard Maggie mutter, "Now, that's what I call action."

Dedication

This book is dedicated to the village of supporters:
God, Husband, Children, Parents, Sibs,
Friends and Family, and NOC chicks.
Special thanks to Bill (aka pea hater),
for the constant push and nagging,
Margret, my grammar police,
Theresa, the encourager,
and Nicole, my patient Editor.

~

In memory of Mike, a member of the H.T.M. Club,
who lost his fight with cancer this year…
your story ideas you pitched to me still make me laugh.

Chapter One

Bing Crosby crooning a Christmas tune on the overhead speaker faded into oblivion as Madison Reynolds' gaze landed on the other occupant in the aisle. Who would have guessed grocery shopping on a Monday night could be this exciting?

She paused, leaned against her cart handle, and rested her chin on her hand. Uncaring she blocked the walkway, her gaze soaked in the man standing in front of the well-stocked cookie shelf.

Even though she'd not seen him in years, she recognized the star of so many of her high school fantasies and dreams. She'd last seen Ryder Sanders on graduation night, over six years ago. She nibbled her lower lip as the memory bombarded her mind. She remembered the nerves and excitement from each of her classmates. The unknown stretched in front of them, the future an open slate.

She shook off her reverie to study the items on the nearby shelf. Her sister wouldn't forgive her if she forgot the purpose of this little grocery run. Where were those coveted Oreos?

The allure was too great. She stole another peek from under her lashes. He looked as yummy as she remembered. His thick black hair tapered down to brush the collar of his leather coat. He studied the shelf before he chose a package to deposit into his cart. Her gaze traveled south to settle on his derriere.

She jerked herself upright. What was she doing? It took her a moment to corral her imagination. Contemplating pinching someone's behind in a grocery store wasn't kosher. Restraint. She needed to find control. Fast.

A voice in her head yelled, *grab the damn cookies, and get out*. Wait. She spied the Oreos. Of course, he stood directly in front of them. Great. She unclenched the cart handle and wiped her damp palms down her sweats. What was the big deal anyway? He wasn't going to remember the fool she made of herself the last time she'd seen him.

A shiver of regret stole down her spine as she recalled the after-graduation celebration at Pilar Beck's house. She'd attended the party with her best friend Zoe Pratt. They'd entered the dimly lit basement to the sounds of laughter and music.

Pilar's parents had outdone themselves. Not only did they have games and music, but also dancing and punch. Curse that beverage. The drink was the bane of her evening.

She rubbed a hand across her brow. This is where her memory always became fuzzy. After she consumed multiple glasses of punch, Zoe overheard some of the boys say they spiked the fruity drink. Her first encounter with alcohol had not gone well. Which may explain why the rest of the evening was a blur.

Spurred by the liquor encouragement coursing through her system, she asked Ryder to dance. He surprised her when he gave her his dimpled grin and said yes. She almost stumbled as the fast tune blasting through the basement changed to a slow melody. One of her fantasies was about to become reality, being held in his arms. The last thing she recalled was his hand settling on her lower back.

Zoe laughingly supplied the details of the evening's end the next day when she'd phoned. Whether prompted by nerves or alcohol, Madison upchucked all over Ryder's shoes. A groan escaped. What a fool she'd made of herself.

Why couldn't time erase the incident from her mind? Curse her pregnant sister's cravings. She rolled her shoulders, straightened, and placed a hand on her fluttering stomach. How could he still have this effect on her? Enough time had passed to diminish this juvenile reaction. Right?

With a mental shake, she looked down at her ratty sweatpants and washed-out sweater. Why do you always run into people you know when your appearance is at its worst? She patted her ponytail. A quick tuck had the stray strands gathered back into the band. At least she hoped they were confined.

What should she say? She stopped a few steps from him. Her nostrils flared as the tantalizing scent of his cologne drifted under her nose. Woodsy. She closed her eyes and inhaled. Man, he smelled divine.

All coherent words scattered in her mind. Forget her bravado from moments before when she planned on speaking. She leaned around him and grabbed a bag of cookies. After placing the package in her cart, she wheeled away with a quick glance over her shoulder.

Ryder Sanders startled at the soft voice behind him saying, "Excuse me." A hand brushed his arm before snagging a bag of cookies. He shifted. "I'm sorry. I didn't realize I blocked you." The woman didn't speak as she strode away, leaving behind a faint trail of a floral scent. He tilted his head as he studied the retreating back. Her chestnut hair skewed up in a messy ponytail swung with each step. Before she rolled out of sight, she paused and glanced back over her shoulder. Her gaze met his and held. Surprise punched him in the stomach. He would swear the shy glance belonged to Madison Reynolds, minus the eyeglasses she'd worn in high school.

He grabbed a final item off the shelf before he wheeled after the woman. At the end of the aisle, he peered about but couldn't see where she'd gone. Had the woman been Madison? Why hadn't she said hello? His search seemed futile as other shoppers blocked his view. He shook his head as his cell vibrated in his pocket. Craning his neck one final time, he gave up and pulled out his phone. "Hi, Alex. What's up?"

"Are you still at the store?"

Wheeling his cart to the next aisle, he shuffled aside so he didn't block anyone. "Yes. Let me guess, you're adding to my list?"

A deep chuckle sounded through the speaker. "Your girl is begging for food. I gave her what we had at the office, but by tomorrow she'll be on the warpath if she doesn't have her kibble."

"Duly noted. I will grab a bag while I'm here."

"Thanks. See you tomorrow."

The tabloids didn't hold his attention as he waited in line at the checkout. His mind wandered back to the woman he'd spotted earlier. Madison sported short hair all through high school and wore glasses, but the lady in the cookie aisle had neither. Although the hairstyle was longer, the color was the same.

"Sir?"

The clerk behind the conveyor blinked at him in expectation. A quick glimpse down he realized his groceries were rung up and bagged. He retrieved his wallet. "Sorry. I'm distracted tonight."

On the drive home, big fluffy snowflakes began to fall. He switched on the wipers. The weatherman finally got the forecast correct. He was glad he didn't have any further activities to attend tonight.

Balancing the grocery bags in his arms, he unlocked his front door. Heat caressed his chilled cheeks as he stepped into the foyer. The outside temperature had dropped while he'd been inside the store. This weather reminded him why he'd outgrown living in a condo. When he finally made a home purchase, a fireplace was one of the amenities required.

A gust of wind rattled the kitchen window as he unpacked the food and put it away. Did he want to prepare the steak he'd bought at the store? Or be lazy and watch the game on television with something simple?

The decision was made for him as his stomach rumbled. Had he skipped lunch today? He didn't remember taking a break. He made short work of making a sandwich and retrieved a beer from the refrigerator before settling on the couch.

The sports announcer's voice faded into the background as he finished his meal and sipped his beer. With his head resting against the cushions, his thoughts turned back to Madison Reynolds.

Chapter Two

Madison heaved a sigh as she pulled into her sister's drive. She eased her white-knuckled grip from the steering wheel and turned off the ignition. The snow was coming down hard and beginning to accumulate on the streets.

Now safely back at Maggie's, she relived the embarrassing actions she'd exhibited at the store. She groaned as she rested her forehead against the wheel. Like a coward, she'd hidden behind a holiday display until Ryder moved away.

A chill stole over her as she eased back in her seat. She was such an idiot. Would saying a simple hello have killed her? The moment he'd glanced at her, she'd been transported back to the awkward teen from years gone by. And wow. Before she fled, the small glimpse she'd taken of the rugged Ryder of today with his five o'clock shadow put the clean-shaven high school image to shame.

A choked laugh escaped. Why did he have such an effect on her? Her mind flashed back. The crush she had on him wrecked her high school years. A single good morning in the halls would have her tongue-tied and her stomach in knots for hours. She shook her head in disgust. His girlfriend, Pilar, noticed her true feelings. There was no way she couldn't have known. The glares she'd aim in her direction spoke volumes.

What a hopeless geek, even after all these years.

With a quick inhale, she took a calming breath. Pilar and Ryder were probably already married and had one or two children. She'd tried a few years ago to find him on social media, but her search hadn't produced any results.

Sitting in her car obsessing over the past didn't accomplish anything. With a glance out the windshield, she noted the lack of Christmas decorations adorning Maggie's house. A quick peek at the neighbor to the right hosted a huge blow-up reindeer with blue twinkling icicle lights dangling off their roof. The house to their left had a large nativity with white lights glimmering in the bushes. She mentally added decorating tasks as one of the projects she needed to take care of while she was here.

She frowned as she remembered her brother-in-law, Jim, calling last Friday night. She'd panicked when he told her the doctor placed Maggie on bed rest as a precaution with her pregnancy. Everything had seemed fine at Thanksgiving, so the news filled her with alarm.

Bright and early on Monday she talked to Frank, her boss, and requested time off to come help Maggie while their parents were on a cruise. She'd spent the morning clearing items off her desk and talked to her assistant about what projects were in the works. A few hours later she'd arrived to find her sister throwing a pity party for herself, and her nephew worried about why mommy cried. Jim left with reluctance shortly after she arrived to attend his business conference. He was one of the presenters and couldn't miss the convention. He'd been relieved to hear she was on her way when she'd phoned. His sigh of relief still echoed in her ears.

A shiver snaked down her spine as she exited the car. The slight cold breeze had also picked up since she'd left for the store. She turned and retrieved the groceries. As she opened the front door, she smiled at Taggert, her four-year-old nephew, playing with his Hot Wheels cars in the living room. The noise level rivaled any monster rally she'd ever seen. A sports car took a flying leap from the couch to the coffee table and a big explosion noise emerged from his lips. She strode toward the kitchen to deposit the sack on the countertop. He was such a delightful boy. She was excited to spend time with him while she visited.

"Maggie, I'm back." She chuckled as her sister's squeal of delight carried down the hallway.

"After you put away the groceries, could you bring the bag of Oreos? Please." The pleasantry at the end of her request seemed added as an afterthought.

Maggie's demands made her chuckle. She'd only been here half a day and already sent on a cookie run. Oh, the power a craving held over a pregnant woman.

As she tore open the bag, she made her way down the hall. "Sure. You'll get your cookies as long as you can spare one for your favorite sibling." She entered the bedroom and rattled the bag. "Who wants an Oreo?" Maggie sat in bed with her favorite sweatshirt on and hair scrunched up in a sloppy ponytail. Her eyes were still a little puffy from her crying bout she'd had earlier, but there was a twinkle in her gaze now, which was previously missing.

She frowned, leaned forward, and made a grab for the bag. "Don't provoke the pregnant woman. Teasing me will not end well for you."

Madison held the bag away. "Threats? Don't bite the hand who retrieved the cookies for you."

With an undignified huff, Maggie leaned back against the pillows and crossed her arms. "Oh, please give them to me already."

A twinge of guilt pricked her conscious at her sister's defeated air. She sat down on the edge of the bed and extended the bag in offering.

The pouty expression upon her face disappeared for a brief moment before being replaced by a frown of confusion. "What are these?"

What was she talking about? She glanced at the package and groaned. She'd grabbed the wrong cookies. The bag contained Oreos, but instead of the white icing inside, a red color peeked out from between the chocolate layers. "Oops. I guess I grabbed the wrong ones."

"You had one job. Just one." Maggie examined the cookie she held before she took a bite. The crunch filled the silent space between them. She swallowed before stating, "Well, you goofed. But these are pretty good." She examined the cookie she held. "And festive. They are Christmas wedged in between a couple of layers of chocolate. I guess you are forgiven."

Maddy wiped her hand across her brow. "Whew. I almost failed my first assignment on operation pregnant sister watch."

She finished chewing. "What took you so long at the store? You've been gone for hours and hours. And then you bring me the wrong bag."

A chuckle escaped as she glanced at her watch. "Since when does thirty minutes equate to hours and hours? Exaggerate much?"

Maggie shrugged her shoulders. "Time drags when confined."

She couldn't begin to understand her sister's frustration. She'd always been so active. This confinement truly was hard on her. "Should I even broach the subject of how you're feeling?"

A sheepish expression spread across her face as she lifted another cookie and took a bite. "I'm sorry I snapped at you. I'm a lot better now you've given me my fix." She examined the cookie. "Or something close to what I requested."

She watched Maggie twist, dissect, and devour the center icing before asking, "When do you go back to the doctor?"

Pausing in her ministrations she replied, "On Wednesday."

"What time is your appointment?" Madison snagged a cookie while her sister was distracted.

"Hey. Stop it!"

The death glare leveled in her direction made her giggle.

"We need to arrive at the doctor's office by ten. Plenty of time to wrestle Taggert into clothes."

Another thing she'd learned this afternoon. Taggert still sported his jammies when she'd arrived. Talking him into getting dressed had taken her almost an hour. "Don't worry about him. I've got this." She shifted to steal another cookie, but Maggie grabbed the package away before she could confiscate another one.

"Why didn't you buy your own stash? They may not be the ones I requested, but these are mine."

She held up her hands in self-defense. "Gotcha. I

won't try to steal any more."

Her distrustful glare relaxed as she placed a hand on her arm. "Maddy. Thank you. I appreciate you being here and helping us out during this time. You're a lifesaver."

She patted her hand. "I'm happy I can help."

"I know I'm going to give you a hard time, so I apologize now. But I'm pleased you are able to help."

Her heart warmed at her words. "I'm glad to lend a hand. You didn't tell mom and dad you've been put on bed rest, did you?"

"Are you kidding me?" She shook her head. "They saved for years for this cruise. I don't want them to ditch their trip." Rubbing her burgeoning belly, she stated, "Besides, they will be back in plenty of time before these two munchkins make their appearance. We're not going to sweat the small stuff."

She rose from the bed. "If you're not worried, then neither am I."

"Jim called earlier. He arrived at the conference okay. But he couldn't hide the anxiety in his voice. I think he's worried enough for both of us."

A chuckle escaped as she shook her head. "I can only imagine. Do you not remember how he acted when you were pregnant the first time around? Now you carry twins, his panic is two-fold."

Maggie groaned. "The memory is one I've placed in the dark recesses of my mind."

"Having any luck?"

A snort emerged from her lips. "No."

"His paranoia is a little justified this time." She held up her hand and ticked off a few points with her fingers. "First, you were placed on bed rest. Second, his conference is out of town. Third, mom and dad aren't here to help. Fourth, to top off the circumstances, he was unsure if I'd be able to help. I think maybe you should cut the poor guy a break."

A groan emerged and she shook her head. "Okay. You do make several valid arguments."

"Of course, I do." She fluffed her ponytail with a quick flick of her hand. "Now who's the smarter one?"

"Don't let the compliment go to your head."

"Too late." Madison pivoted toward the door. "Do you need anything else before I go start dinner?"

Maggie lowered the cookie she'd been about to devour. "I guess I shouldn't eat any more of these. Until after I've eaten a nutritious meal." She quirked a brow. "Please tell me you didn't base your food choice on Taggert's suggestions. I'm not sure I can face a hot dog and mac n' cheese again so soon. Jim tried this weekend, but bless his soul, he's not much of a cook."

She lifted a hand and touched her chest. "I rank better than Jim? Have you forgotten the stuffing incident at Thanksgiving? Now I know this pregnancy is messing with your mind."

Maggie slapped the palm of her hand against her forehead. "Ugh. The smell took a day and a half to get out of my kitchen."

A grimace traveled down her back. "Sorry. Well, you can breathe easy tonight. I don't plan on having dressing on the menu. I am making spaghetti and meatballs."

A sigh of relief, or maybe delight, escaped her sister's lips. "Your specialty. I remember."

Her mind wandered back to Ryder. She nibbled on her bottom lip. Should she ask her nosy sister about him? Maybe confiding could wait and she should ask Google. The search engine may be a simpler choice with less guff.

Maggie squinted her eyes. "Out with the question."

Confusion flooded her mind. "What?"

"Whenever you bite your lip, I know you're trying to decide whether or not to tell me something. So, what's the scoop?"

Could she be read so easily? "Oh, you think you're so smart?"

"Of course. I'm the oldest."

Stopping at the nearby dresser, she trailed her fingers over the items on top. "You're going to think I'm stupid for asking."

Maggie leaned forward in the bed and waved her hands impatiently. "Come on, spit your question out."

In the reflection of the dresser mirror, she met her gaze. "Ryder Sanders was at the grocery store, and I wondered if you are aware of what he does these days."

A cheeky grin broke upon her face. "Ah, the ol' high school crush? You tell me. You're the one who ran into him at the store."

Shrugging her shoulders, she picked up a bottle of perfume and sniffed. Nice. "Well, I didn't actually converse with him."

A disgusted sigh escaped her lips. "Madison, seriously? What are we going to do with you?"

With a turn toward Maggie, she smiled. "Love me unconditionally?"

"Too late. I already do."

"I know."

The cookie package rattled as she closed it firmly. "I've been listening to you for years going on and on about Ryder. All they've ever been were empty words. I think the time has come for action"

Crossing the few feet to the bed, she placed a calming hand upon her shoulder. "All right, Momma Bear, don't get in a huff. I didn't mean to get you all excited."

Maggie settled back down against her pillow and assessed her. "Now I understand why you got the wrong cookies. You were distracted, weren't you?"

Busted. She let her gaze drop from her sister's cool one. "Maybe."

An aggravated sigh sounded from the bed. "I've never understood your lack of self-confidence. Take a peek in the mirror sometime. You are a beautiful young woman. You need to realize the fact. And to add insult to injury, you got the long, beautiful legs." With a groan, she indicated her legs, "Unlike my shorter stubbier ones."

Maddy turned back to the mirror above the dresser and studied her reflection. A blush stained her cheeks at the compliment. "I don't know why I doubt myself. If you could shed some light on the subject, Freud, I would be internally grateful."

Smiling she responded, "Freud, sounds good. After all, I'm the one with the brains in this family."

Groaning she muttered, "Great. I've created a monster." Suddenly she realized how quiet the house had become. "Do you hear that?"

Maggie shrugged. "I don't hear anything."

An accusing finger flew in the direction of the bed. "Exactly. Your mother radar is definitely off. I need to check on Taggert. The house seems too quiet."

As she shuffled toward the door, Maggie

interrupted her departure, "He's an architect."

Maddy frowned and twirled around to tease her sister. "I didn't realize my nephew was so talented and at such a young age."

"Don't be such a smart butt. You know I meant Ryder, you idiot."

"Hmmm. An architect." She crossed her arms and leaned against the doorjamb. "Come on, out with the details."

Deep in thought, she tapped a finger against her lip. "I think I remember reading in the paper he'd partnered with a guy named Alex Fisher. Their offices are downtown. They built the new strip shopping area south of town and various housing additions."

Should she ask the question rattling around in her mind? She bit her lip again. "Um. Do you know if he married Pilar or if he's single?"

Her sister rolled her eyes in a dramatic fashion. "We live in Cedar Bend, Colorado, not Hollywood. The *National Inquirer* has yet to publish the information."

"Hey…" She shrugged her shoulders. "I figured since you are the brains of the family you would know."

"Flattery. Skillfully played."

"Thank you," she said with a smile.

Maggie tilted her head. "You know his business partner Alex is single. Now he is a dreamboat! I would go after Alex if Ryder isn't available."

"Uh, uh, uh." She wagged a finger at her sister. "You had better watch those roving eyes, or I will tell Jim."

"Hey, I wouldn't be doing my sisterly duty if I let an opportunity slip through your fingers. Besides, I can scrutinize the menu, I just can't order. My husband knows my flaws."

A laugh exploded from her lips as she turned to exit the room. "Opportunity is what you call it these days? Are you sure what you are doing isn't matchmaking?"

Her sister's voice followed her down the hallway. "Call it what you want. I still say the period for talk is over. It's time for action."

Chapter Three

Ryder silenced the television. The game was over, and if anyone asked, he wouldn't be able to say who won. All evening he'd wrestled with why Madison hadn't talked to him at the store. He leaned forward with his arms on his thighs. In high school, she'd always been quiet and shy. It seemed she hadn't outgrown the trait.

Not sure why, he rose minutes later to search for his high school yearbook. The spare room closet didn't produce any positive results. Where had he stashed it? He'd only been in this condo for less than a year and there were still boxes he hadn't unpacked. He made his way into the attached garage. Along the wall, a stack of containers reached almost to the ceiling. Was his touch of nostalgia worth tackling the job he'd been putting off?

Upon opening the third box, he found what he sought. A light layer of dust had somehow seeped in to coat the contents. He stepped around the previous boxes he'd abandoned and strode into the house. A glance at the wall clock indicated it wasn't too late. He placed the carton on his coffee table and settled on the couch. With a swipe of his hand, he dusted off the yearbook, opened it, and settled back against the cushions.

****

Madison stood at the kitchen sink washing the

evening dishes. The house was blessedly silent. Taggert had gone to bed a couple of hours ago with great reluctance, and Maggie watched TV in her room with her eyes closed.

To ease her tense muscles, she shrugged her shoulders. She'd survived her first day as a helpmate. Taggert was such a live wire. Her sister wouldn't be able to cope on her own with Jim away.

A loud bang clanged outside the window. She nearly dropped the dish she held. The noise came from the backyard. Heart pounding, she dried her hands on a nearby towel. Was the racket an intruder? She eased away from the window and glanced about for her phone. Now where had she put the dang thing?

Maggie appeared in the kitchen doorway hiding a yawn behind the back of her hand.

"Mags. Did you hear the noise coming from the backyard?" She glanced about once more. "I'm calling nine-one-one as soon as I locate where I laid my blasted phone."

Unfazed, her sister made her way to the refrigerator and opened the door. She didn't utter a word as she poured herself a glass of milk.

Was her sister sleepwalking? "Did you hear me? Someone is in the backyard." Panic bubbled in her chest like a carbonated drink being exposed to air.

Maggie rinsed her glass and shuffled back toward the hall. "I'm listening. But the noise isn't anything to get worked up over. It's Flynn and Mabel."

Which was worse? Maggie naming the intruders? Or they visited enough to have names? "Mags?"

With a wave of her hand she stated, "Go ahead and call the police, but they will tell you the same thing. It's

Flynn and Mabel. They have a reputation in this neighborhood."

Hands on her hips she demanded, "Care to share with me who Flynn and Mabel are?" Even though her sister wasn't alarmed, the wave of panic still hadn't subsided within her chest.

Maggie giggled. "A couple of bandits." Her smile disappeared. Maybe her fear finally registered with her. "They are raccoons. I'm sure you will catch a glimpse of them while you're here visiting. I'm going back to bed. Night."

Okay, just breathe, she reprimanded herself. Raccoons. She frowned as confusion crowded into her brain. Weren't they supposed to hibernate this time of year? Another noise echoed from the back of the house. What were they doing back there? Having a neighborhood block party? She eased over to the back door and flipped on the yard light. A loud clang followed, and as she peered out the window, two fuzzy backsides scurried across the lawn. "Well, hello, Flynn and Mabel. I'm not sure I'm happy to meet you, but I'm glad you're not an intruder."

As her heart rate returned to normal, she began turning off the lights and made her way to the guest bedroom. She brushed her teeth and stared into the mirror studying her reflection. Had Ryder recognized her? Regret edged in. Why hadn't she said hello? Conversation would surely have flowed after a simple greeting.

Her laptop beckoned as she emerged from the bathroom. Would Maggie's information help her solve her curiosity about Ryder? Sitting cross-legged on the bed, she stretched to grasp her nearby computer. After a few moments of searching, she found an article in the local newspaper covering the ribbon-cutting event for the new strip mall. Bingo. There he stood smiling for the camera. Her gaze was drawn to Ryder automatically before she noticed the other man in the picture. This must be his business partner. Her sister didn't lie. He was a handsome man. The smile slipped from her lips as she noticed the woman with her arm threaded through Ryder's. Pilar.

The image couldn't make the scenario any plainer. She was still part of his life. Frustrated over her fascination for him, she shut her laptop with more force than necessary.

Aggravated, she punched her pillow, turned the light off, and flopped her head down.

Chapter Four

"Aunt Maddy, can you add a smiley face to my pancake?"

Hiding a yawn behind a hand, she shook her head and tried to focus on the conversation Taggert manipulated. "Sorry, squirt. What did you ask?"

A huge sigh shook his little body. "Are you not payin' attention?"

The serious expression upon his face made her chuckle. "You caught me. I wasn't."

He climbed up on the stool next to where she worked. "Can I have a smiley face on my pancake?"

Before meeting his gaze, she flipped the flapjack. "Are you sure your breakfast is happy? He seems sad to me."

A funny expression crossed his face as he studied the pan. "Put a smile on it. Then the pancake will be happy."

Reaching out, she ruffled his hair and tried not to take offense of his opinion of her cooking. She opened the refrigerator and examined the contents. "Let's see if we can find a smile in the fridge." A quick scan inside presented a can of whipped cream and some chocolate chips. "You're in luck." She flipped the pancake out of the skillet, shook the can of cream, and added hair. As he giggled, she added a few chips for eyes and then a line of chips for a mouth. "Wa-la. What do you think?"

He jumped down from the chair, flung his arms around her legs, and looked up at her. "You are the best aunt ever."

"Thanks, kiddo. Now climb back up and eat your breakfast before it gets cold." She laughed as he attacked his breakfast with gusto.

"You're going to spoil him, ya know."

Twirling about, she opened her mouth to admonish Maggie for being out of bed, but was halted.

Her sister put her hand up. "Bathroom break, don't go all ballistic on me."

"Look, Mom. See what Aunt Maddy made me?"

"Way cool, Tiger, but don't talk with your mouth full."

Maggie scrutinized her as she rubbed her belly, retrieved a glass, and filled it with water. "What do you have on the agenda for today's activities?"

Lifting the pan away from the burner, she extinguished the flame. "Taggert and I could get a tree and some decorations. Your house and yard look like the Grinch stole your Christmas."

Around another mouthful of food, he gave a whoop of joy. He swallowed before asking. "A real tree? Cool. Can we, Mom?"

"What a great idea. A few decorations around here would make the house appear a little more festive."

She nudged her sister's shoulder. "If your mom behaves, maybe she can lounge on the couch and watch us decorate."

A smile tugged at her mouth as she shuffled toward the kitchen doorway. "I can't think of a better way to participate." She glanced backward. "Thank you, Maddy."

She flashed a thumbs-up signal to Taggert. "Okay, buddy, wash your hands, and let's get you bundled up."

****

Ryder's eyes watered as he stared at his computer. The current drawing blurred before he blinked and shook his head. "I'm sorry. Did you say something?"

His business partner, Alex Fisher, crossed the office to stand by his desk with a smile upon his face. "I asked why you're so distracted this morning."

Lacing his fingers behind his head, he leaned back in his chair. "Sorry. I guess I hadn't realized."

"What's up? Problems with one of our projects?"

"No. We're good." His gaze met Alex's. "Last night at the store there was a woman there who reminded me of a classmate. I've been sitting here pondering what she is doing these days." He shrugged. "I guess I was deep in thought."

"Have you tried searching social media?"

He leaned forward in his chair. "You know I don't bother with those sites."

"Sometimes messing with those sites gets answers. Come over to my computer, and we'll search on my account."

Did he want to attempt to find answers? The previous evening, he spent hours browsing the yearbook. He still didn't understand why, but the candid shots had transported him back to pleasant memories from his younger days. He still believed Madison was the woman at the store. But why was he obsessing about her whereabouts?

"Ryder?"

With a shake of his head, he brought himself back to the present. "Okay, I want to know." He rose and crossed the room to stand behind Alex at his desk.

"Let's try Facebook first." A few clicks later he asked, "What is the lady's name?"

"Madison Reynolds." He scrutinized Alex as his fingers flew over the keys. Moments later her smiling face appeared.

He glanced over his shoulder. "Is this your classmate?"

Turning, he grabbed a nearby chair and pulled it close. "Yes." In the picture, she wore her hair longer and once again didn't wear glasses, but there was no mistake. It was the woman from the store the previous night.

Alex clicked on the profile. "Let's see what we can find out."

Her page popped up, and the first photo was of her with a little boy. The child's arms hugged her neck as he smiled for the picture. A bubble of disappointment coursed through him as he noted the post was made yesterday.

"Why aren't you happy?"

How could he explain his regret when he didn't understand his disappointment himself? He shrugged his shoulders. "She's obviously attached and has a child."

Alex snorted, tilted his head, and studied him. "You don't know how to do this social media stuff. Did you not see her status to the left?"

His gaze swung to the small box he indicated. She was employed in Colorado Springs at a bank as a loan officer. She had attended Cedar Bend High School and was listed as single. The word made him smile and lean back in satisfaction.

Alex shook his head. "Is this curiosity more than wanting to catch up with a classmate?"

After he scratched his chin, he shrugged. "Maybe. She was always so quiet in school. I wanted to get to know her, but she treated me like I had the plague." He chuckled as a previous memory came to mind. "Actually, the last time we were together, she puked on my brand-new shoes."

Another snort emerged from Alex's lips. "Talk about leaving a lasting impression."

"The incident is imprinted in my memory. If I remember, Pilar was more irritated because the event happened in her parent's basement at the after-graduation party." He rose from the chair. "Thanks for searching for me."

"No problem. What do you plan on doing with the information?"

In a couple of strides, he retrieved his coat from the back of his chair and shrugged into it. "Well, this little search proves Madison was at the store last night. I need to find out how long she's in town and hope I can connect with her somehow." He zipped his jacket. "I'm going after a coffee. Do you want one?"

He pointed at the machine in the corner. "My coffee not good enough for you?"

A small shudder traveled down his spine. "I think your brew could stand up in a corner by itself. No offense."

Alex chuckled and placed a hand over his heart. "I'm wounded, but I guess I don't blame you."

Chapter Five

Madison hummed jingle bells as she followed behind her skipping nephew. She breathed in the soft pine fragrance permeating the air. Their errand to find outdoor decorations ended in success. Taggert picked out a couple of laser lights to reflect on the house. One reflected snowflakes, and the other displayed Santa with his reindeer guiding his sleigh. She also bought a small crate to convert into a manger and a blow-up Santa.

"How 'bout this one, Aunt Maddy?"

The reindeer antlers she'd donned jiggled as she tilted her head to study his choice. "I don't know. The tree seems a little lopsided. Are you sure about this one?"

His little body shook with the huge sigh he released. "It's perfect."

She nodded and took his hand in her own. "Okay. The scrawny Charlie Brown tree comes home with us."

"Mom will love this one."

His enthusiasm made her smile. "Sure she will squirt. You did a great job of picking." He beamed at her praise. "Let's pay for your tree."

The older gentleman at the front of the lot smiled at them. "Can I help you?"

"This young man has found a tree. We need to pay and make arrangements for delivery."

The attendant grimaced, and his smile dimmed. "I'm sorry. I can handle your purchase, but our delivery person is out sick with the flu. I'm not sure when he will be back to make deliveries."

A glance at the tree made her question whether it would fit on top of her compact car. Could they strap the pine onto her roof with the man's help?

"Can I lend a hand?"

Startled, she spun around, and her gaze encountered the dancing brown eyes of Ryder Sanders.

"Hi, Madison."

Play it cool, and don't make a fool of yourself. "Hey, Ryder." She cringed. Was that croak emerging her voice? The pep talk taking place in her brain hadn't registered with her speech.

His gaze swept over her before his lips quirked into a smile. "I have a truck if you'd like me to deliver the tree for you and your son."

Son? Oh, Taggert. Goodness, he'd rattled her. She'd forgotten her nephew holding her hand. Her cheeks heated with embarrassment. A nervous chuckle escaped. "Oh, this little tyke is my nephew, Taggert. My sister's son. You remember Maggie, don't you?"

"Sure." He squatted down to peer at Taggert at eye level. He switched the coffee cup to his other hand before shaking her nephew's hand. "It's nice to meet you, young man."

Like a grown-up, he accepted the offering. "Hi. Are you Aunt Maddy's boyfriend?"

A chuckle escaped as he glanced up at her and winked. "Well, I am a boy and we're friends. So, I guess I am."

A sliver of shock traveled down her spine. Ryder

Sanders winked. She wanted to pinch herself to make sure she wasn't hallucinating. His eyes were as warm as hot fudge drizzled on a sundae. What had he asked? She remembered his question before her brain short-circuited. Oh, yeah, the dilemma with the tree.

Rising to his feet he asked, "Are you okay?" He took a quick step back. "You're not going to throw up, are you?"

Great. Her worst fear realized. The man she fantasized about believed she was a puke risk. She chuckled and shook her head. "No. You've already had the privilege."

His mouth quirked. "You've got to admit, the event left an impression."

A tug on her hand sent her focus downward to her nephew. "Is the tree coming home with us?"

Her gaze swung back to Ryder's. "Thanks for the help. Are you sure it's not an inconvenience? I'd hate to bother you if you don't have time."

"It's no trouble at all. I wouldn't have offered otherwise." He consulted his watch. "I have the time."

Those dang butterflies emerged from their cocoons in her stomach as he smiled again. Her focus was off. Had he asked another question? "I'm sorry. What did you ask?" His eyes danced with a hint of amusement, making them twinkle. She hoped he didn't realize the effect he had on her.

"The address? Where do I need to deliver the tree?"

A wave of heat traveled to her cheeks. "An address would be helpful. Sorry. Maggie lives at two ten Ponderosa Drive."

He nodded and murmured the address back. "I

know exactly where to find you."

Chills raced down her arms. Was it her imagination, or did his words hold a hidden promise? Breaking eye contact, she asked Taggert, "You ready to go home?" At his nod, she turned and spoke over her shoulder. "We'll meet you there in a few minutes, and thanks again for the help."

Ryder kept an eye on her as she helped the little boy into his car seat in a compact a short distance away. He'd only stepped out for coffee. Now he'd get to spend time with her. Luck was on his side this morning.

Taking a sip from his coffee cup, he grimaced at the now cold coffee.

"I have a trash can here if you are through with your drink."

He thanked the tree attendant before retrieving his cell from his coat pocket. Alex answered after a couple of rings. "Ryder. What's up? Did you get lost?"

A chuckle escaped. "I guess I did."

"Did they have to go to Colombia to pick your coffee beans?"

"Always the comedian, aren't you? No. I'm delivering a Christmas tree for a friend and will be back in the office later."

"Hmmm. Is this friend male or female?"

"Why does the gender matter?"

Alex's chuckle echoed through the receiver. "Definitely female."

"Well." Pausing, he cleared his throat. "I'm going to pick out a tree for the office while I'm at the lot."

"Great. It's about time you got into the spirit of the season."

The bubble of excitement invading his body was

either the Christmas spirit like Alex had suggested, or credited to a chance encounter with a certain female.

Chapter Six

"Mom. We're home."

Madison shook her head in wonder at Taggert's energy as he tore down the hallway to the back bedroom. She wondered how her sister was going to survive adding twins to the mix. She entered the bedroom in time to hear him tell her Aunt Maddy's boyfriend would deliver the tree they bought.

"Do you have something to tell me?" Her sister quirked a brow and met her gaze. "Because I swear you didn't have a boyfriend when you left the house this morning. I guess you took my time-for-action advice seriously. Good for you."

Holding up a hand, she shook her head. "Before you get too excited, the boyfriend status isn't what you think. The lot attendant who delivers is out sick, and Ryder happened by and offered to bring the tree we bought to the house."

A smirk graced her sister's face. "Ryder, huh?" She swung her feet off the bed.

Madison frowned at her actions. "What do you think you're doing?"

"I'm going to the couch to watch you decorate and to check out your boyfriend when he arrives." An evil chuckle escaped her lips as she exited the bedroom.

A groan escaped past her lips. Great. Just great. Before she made her way down the hallway, the doorbell rang.

Upon entering the room, she caught Maggie peeking through the blinds. "Okay. I'd forgotten how yummy he looks. Your boyfriend is here."

"Shhh. Zip your mouth. He'll hear you." Maggie shrugged her shoulders and giggled. Maddy pointed to the couch. "Sit. Get off your feet."

A grumble escaped, but she did as she asked. "I'm going, I'm going." She made herself comfortable before a grin broke out on her face. "By the way. I love how your reindeer ears accent your outfit. Quite chic."

With a gasp, she tried to snatch the springy ears off her head and cringed when her hair got caught. She'd forgotten they were on her head. No wonder Ryder viewed her with such amusement at the tree lot. It would be hard to have a serious conversation with someone who sported a silly child's toy upon her head. Tears sprang to her eyes as the spring further twisted in her hair making the tangle of the antlers worse. Defeated, she opened the door. What did the impression she made matter anyway? She lost the chance of making a good impact years ago.

"Tree delivery." He tilted his head and laughter bubbled from his lips. "Um, your ears are hanging low, Rudolph."

Trying to control her tears, she attempted again to remove the headpiece. Dang it, she made the situation worse. "Ha ha. Everyone is such the comedian today. The stupid things got stuck when I wanted to take them off."

He took a step forward.

She swallowed hard and stuttered. "What are you doing?"

"Lending a hand."

Her gaze collided with his before she lowered her eyes. The brush of his fingers against her own as he moved her hand away had her holding her breath. With a gentleness she hadn't expected, he worked at untangling the spring. The tantalizing scent of his cologne drifted under her nose and she inhaled deeply. Her nerve endings tingled in awareness at his nearness. Who cared if the antlers were permanently attached. She didn't want him to stop running his fingers through her hair. But all good things must come to an end. She sighed as a few minutes later he stepped back and held up the headband. "You're free."

"Thank you." Was that her breathy voice?

"No problem." He withdrew his hands, cupped them together, and blew into them.

"Don't you have gloves? I'm sorry. I shouldn't have made you wait out here in the cold. Come in before your fingers fall off."

He chuckled and blew into his hands again. "I wondered if I would be invited in." He retrieved the tree propped against the house and followed her inside. "Where are we putting this beauty?"

A snort escaped her lips. She leaned in and whispered, "We both know there were prettier trees on the lot, but I didn't want to disappoint Taggert. He picked this one."

He put a finger to his lips. "Shhh. This pine has feelings you know."

She forced her gaze away from his lips before whispering, "Sorry. I didn't mean to tree shame." She gestured with her hand. "Right here in front of the window should be a good spot."

Her sister cleared her throat getting their attention. "Hi, Ryder."

He eased the tree down to the floor before he greeted her. "Hi, Maggie. I haven't seen you in years."

"Yeah, probably since Mr. Rooks' history class when you always got in trouble for drawing during class."

He laughed and shook his head in wonder. "I still don't know how I passed his class."

"All your doodling paid off. Congratulations on your architectural firm. You've done well for yourself."

"Thank you. I enjoy what I'm doing."

Maggie shifted to rise. "Can I get you something to drink?"

Madison pointed and commanded, "Don't you dare. Stay put."

Her sister crisscrossed her arms over her chest. "See how she acts? Give her a reason to boss her elders, and she takes full advantage of the situation."

Taggert tugged on his pant leg. "The babies aren't behaving. Mom has to take it easy."

Easing down on a knee, he leveled his gaze with Taggert's. "Have you been a big help?"

"Yup." Everyone laughed at Taggert's aggressive nod.

"I know you picked out the gorgeous tree I delivered. What else have you done?"

"I helped Aunt Maddy make smiley face pancakes for breakfast. They were cool."

"I bet." He ruffled his hair. "Pancakes with a smile are my favorites too."

A huge grin lit his face, showing a gap where a tooth used to reside. "Maybe Aunt Maddy can make you some for breakfast sometime."

A wolfish smirk appeared upon his face before he met her gaze and winked. "I'd enjoy trying them."

The look caused a strangled choke to stall in Madison's throat. Was that a smoldering look cast in her direction? She wasn't an expert. An image that popped into her head made her squirm. Ryder appeared bare-chested lounging in her bed with a breakfast tray nearby. Had he envisioned the same scenario as she did? The second wink of the morning also threw her. He kneeled on her sister's living room floor flirting with her, if she wasn't mistaken. This dream was getting good. Her attention snapped back to Taggert as he asked him to stay and help them decorate the tree. "Oh, Tag, honey, I'm sure he has to get back to work. We've taken up too much of his time already."

Ryder rose and tugged his phone from his pocket to examine the screen for a few moments. "Actually, I'm free for a couple of hours." He shrugged out of his coat and rubbed his hands together. "Put me to work."

Maggie chuckled from the couch. "I like his can-do attitude."

Madison shook her head. She still couldn't believe he was here, and now her nephew had talked him into helping decorate their tree. "Maggie. Taggert and I found some cool yard ornaments. I can't wait for you to see them."

Taggert ran over to the couch. "Mom, we got a Santa. He blows up like a balloon."

Maggie shook her head. "I hope you didn't go overboard, Maddy. I agreed to put a little bit of festive in the yard, not some gaudy display."

A hand rose in innocence and fluttered to cover her

heart. "You wound me."

"Drama Queen."

She stuck her tongue out before saying, "I learned from the best." Her gaze met Ryder's amused one. "Truly. I learned the theatrics from her."

He held up his hands. "I'm not getting in the middle of this one."

Maggie muttered, "Smart man."

"Mom, we also bought some fancy string stuff."

At her quizzical expression, Maddy clarified, "Tinsel garland."

"It's pretty, Mom. It's red and gold."

Maggie gave him a hug. "I can't wait to see what you bought."

"Okay, it's time to get this decorating party started." She rubbed her hands together. "Where are the tree stand and ornaments stored?" Her sister shifted on the couch. "Don't you dare get up. Just tell me where?"

With a disgusted grunt, she inched back against the cushion. "Fine. They're on the shelves inside the garage. I have marked the boxes. You can't miss them."

"Gotcha. I'll be right back." She fumbled a few seconds to find the light inside the garage before she flipped it on. Did people have their garages this organized? She stared in amazement for a moment before eyeballing the boxes. Maggie had labeled every container. On tiptoes, she grasped the carton labeled ornaments.

"Here, let me help you."

Arms gently nudged her aside to grab the larger box, leaving the smaller one for her to carry. "Thanks."

He paused before going back into the house. A concerned frown marred his brow. "Is Maggie okay?"

His closeness still caused her to pause. Between the winks and the nearness he'd displayed today, her nerves hung by a thread and threatened to go over the edge. "Last week at her appointment her blood pressure was high. The doctor placed her on bed rest as a precaution." She shifted. "Her husband, Jim, is out of town at a conference, and he couldn't get out of attending. So, I asked off from work to come down to help out."

"When is her due date?"

"After Christmas. I think her official due date is in the second week of January."

"So, Aunt Maddy to the rescue?"

She shrugged her shoulders. "Something along those lines."

"I'm sorry about the circumstances, but I'm happy I ran into you." He shifted the box in his arms. "Do you think you'll be in town until Christmas?"

"Actually, that's the plan. I had already asked off work to come home before I received the call from Jim. I'm not due back at work until the fifth."

"Great. What other entertainment do you have planned for Taggert and yourself?"

Her mind blanked as she studied his smile and his words. Was he asking to do more activities with her? "Does everyone still go sledding or tubing down the hill north of town?"

He shrugged his shoulders. "As far as I know they do."

"I believe Taggert would love to go tubing. The snowfall we've received this week would be ideal for the activity."

He tilted his head. "Wow. I don't remember the

last time I went sledding down the hill. Care if I tag along?"

Was he serious? Somehow, someway, she'd traveled to an alternate universe. Ryder wanted to spend time with her. "Don't you have to work?"

"Actually, we're pretty caught up and have slowed down with the holidays around the corner. Besides, I haven't taken a vacation day since we started our business."

"Well, if you're sure you can handle the time off. I don't mind you coming with us."

"Great. It's a date."

His words caused a chill to shimmy down her spine, and the sensation wasn't a bad one. A date. She shouldn't let the giddy tide rising in her body take over. But she couldn't help herself. It took a moment for her to realize her cell rang in her pocket. She wrestled with her box before finding a resting place on her hip. She fished the annoying interruption from her pocket. The caller ID read her brother-in-law's number. "Hi, Jim. What's up?"

His voice reverberated with panic. "Where's Maggie? She's not answering her phone."

"Jim. Take a breath and calm down. Everything is okay. She's on the couch. She must have left her phone in the bedroom. Just a second. I'll hand the phone over." She exited the garage and held out the phone. "Papa bear couldn't get hold of you. Please reassure him you're okay and take the call."

A shared smile passed between her and Ryder who'd followed her in from the garage. "Okay, back to the tree." Lowering her box next to Taggert who sat cross-legged on the floor, she opened the flaps on the container. "I need to get our purchases from the car. Can you start going through this and see what we have in here?" She smiled as her nephew nodded with enthusiasm and dug into the ornaments. "I'll be right back." She retrieved her coat and headed outside to gather the bags from her car. One of the containers started to slide from her hands as she opened the front door.

"Here, let me help." Their fingers collided as he relieved the sack from her before the contents spilled in the foyer.

An infusion of heat warmed her cheeks at the tingle his touch caused. "Thanks."

"Aunt Maddy. The box is empty."

A cascade of ornaments of various sizes and shapes surrounded him. He held up a tangled strand of lights. "I didn't do this. They were already like this."

Madison laughed at his affronted look. "Don't worry. I believe you. Who wants to help me unravel the lights?"

Her sister disconnected her phone call. "Here, let me do those. I shouldn't get too tired from the activity."

She passed the wad of lights over to Maggie. "Did you get Jim calmed down?"

Her gaze met her own. "Yes. I'm glad you answered your phone. He almost drove home because I hadn't answered."

Maddy gave her a reassuring pat on her shoulder. "A few more days and he'll be home." Maggie's eyes teared up before she started to untangle the lights. With a glance about, Madison noted the chaos they'd unleashed in the living room. "Who needs a hot chocolate to help them decorate?"

Taggert raised his arm. "Me."

The grown man sitting beside him copied his actions. "Me too."

At everyone's consent, she stepped into the kitchen to make cocoa. She smiled at the animated one-sided conversation Taggert provided. She peeked around the corner to observe Ryder unnoticed. No matter how his attention made her feel, she needed to remember the situation was fleeting. She had her life in Colorado Springs, and he had his here. With Pilar. She frowned, as she wondered why he hadn't mentioned her?

A few moments later, she carried a tray laden with steaming mugs from the kitchen. Placing her burden on the end table, she quickly passed out each. She took a small sip before asking, "All right, lights lady, how are we coming?"

"Untangled, ma'am." She saluted her with one hand as the other cradled her drink.

She took the strand from her and approached the tree.

"Here, let me help you with those." Again, his hand brushed hers as he took the bundle. The same sensation she'd experienced earlier occurred again as the tingle extended along her fingertips. After a slight hesitation on her part, they worked together, and the lights were soon on. She took a step back and put her hands on her hips. "Now. We are ready for the tinsel garland. Taggert wanted me to buy the icicles, but I hope we purchased the less messy option." With a turn, she rummaged through the bags they'd bought, and opened the package of multicolored garland.

"See mom. I told you it was pretty." He touched the red and gold strand in wonder. "I helped pick it out."

"You have a good eye, Tag."

He beamed at his mom's praise. "Can I help put it on?"

Madison took off the wrapping. "I will have to put on the top part." She tapped the tinsel against his nose, "but you can help on the lower part of the tree."

He gave an excited jump. "All right."

The scent of pine tickled her nose as she stretched to the top and began weaving the tinsel around the tree.

A pair of hands intercepted hers. "Here, hand the strand to me." Ryder relieved her of the garland and worked it back around the tree.

When his fingers brushed her own, she dropped the twine. The decoration hit the ground and rolled a few feet away.

Taggert giggled and chased it down. "I'll get it." He continued to laugh as he raced around the tree with the garland firmly grasped in his hands.

"Wait, Tag." But her warning was called out too late. He'd wound the twine around the tree and caught her and Ryder's legs in the process. She fell against his chest as she lost her footing.

He gripped her upper arms as he steadied her when she teetered on her feet. "Whoa, buddy. I think you need some help." He spoke to Taggert, but his gaze lingered and twinkled as it locked with hers.

A snicker echoed from the direction of the couch. She could swear she overheard Maggie mutter, "Now, that's what I call action."

A wave of heat traveled from her breastbone upward to warm her cheeks. She needed to ease away from his embrace, but Taggert had yet to unravel the garland. If the moment couldn't get any more awkward, his phone vibrated in his front jean pocket.

"Sorry." He leaned back and retrieved his phone.

In the confined space, she read the name displayed on the screen before he answered. Pilar.

"Hey." He was silent a moment while he listened. "Oh. I'm sorry." He glanced at his watch. "Tell Roger I'll meet him there shortly. I lost track of time. I'll be there in about ten minutes." After he pocketed his phone, he addressed Taggert. "Hey, buddy. Can you give me a hand getting us untangled?"

"Do you have to go? The tree isn't done yet."

Her nephew wasn't the only one in the room disappointed. But she hoped she disguised the fact better. "Taggert, Ryder needs to go."

He ruffled his hair. "Don't worry, kiddo. I'll see you soon. I need to get back to work to meet with a client."

"Will you help with the Santa we got at the store?"

He quirked a brow in question.

As soon as they were loose from the tinsel, she removed her hands from his chest with great reluctance. "We bought outdoor decorations and lights for the yard."

"Sure, buddy, if I can."

"Taggert, Ryder has things he has to do and needs to go to work."

They both answered at the same time.

He bent to gaze into Taggert's eyes. "Hey. I don't mind. I'd be happy to help."

She stepped back, putting some distance between them. Wouldn't Pilar be displeased with all the time he'd already spent with them? "You shouldn't keep

Pilar waiting. I'll get your coat."

"Pilar's in Denver."

Was he one of those men who flirted with different women when his girlfriend wasn't around? "Anyway, we don't want to keep you from your work. We've already kept you from your job long enough." She sighed and leaned her forehead against the door after he left.

"Wow. Entertainment at its finest."

She twisted to meet her sister's gaze. Great. She struggled not to groan. Here comes the harassment. "I don't know what you mean." She bent to pick up a Styrofoam ornament, which had escaped from the nearby pile of ornaments.

"Are you kidding me? My eyebrows were singed clear over here from the electric current flowing between the two of you."

"I call what you saw static electricity. From the cold weather."

She rose from the couch. "Honey, keep telling yourself those lies. I'm going to go take a nap. By the way, the tree is beautiful so far."

She threw the Styrofoam bulb at her retreating sister's back.

A chuckle echoed down the hallway. "Missed me."

"Aunt Maddy?"

"Yeah, bud." Tag wore such a serious expression upon his face.

"I like your boyfriend. I hope he comes back."

Chapter Seven

What trouble could a four-year-old with the knowledge of how to use a toaster oven get into? Apparently, a lot. Madison's eyes watered and her lips burned. She grabbed her glass of milk and took a swallow. "Taggert? Are you sure you used cinnamon to make the toast?"

He jumped up and retrieved the spice bottle. "See. Doesn't it say cinnamon?"

Her gaze met her sister's. Both sat at the breakfast nook trying to mask their laughter. He'd worked so hard. The spice he held did start with a c, but the similarities ended there. "Well, buddy." She cleared her throat and took another sip of milk. "Kudos for getting the beginning letter correct. But this isn't cinnamon. This bottle is cayenne pepper."

"Oh." A crestfallen expression crossed his features. "What's it used for?"

Maggie put her teacup down. "I use the spice when I make food like tacos."

"The hot ones? I like those."

"I know you do, bud." Her sister patted his hand. "Go brush your teeth. We need to leave soon."

Laughter bubbled from Madison's lips. "Bless his heart. He tried."

Maggie grimaced. "His cooking skills could rival Jim's."

"He's definitely a chip off the ol' block." She rose, picked up the leftover toast, and tossed them in the nearby trash bin.

"Why are you dressed up? You hope to run into a certain someone?"

She smoothed a hand down her skirt. "No. I've spent enough time in sweats and jeans the last few days. I wanted to dress up for your appointment." She sat back down at the table. "Besides, he's still involved with Pilar if his phone call yesterday afternoon proved anything."

"Not necessarily. There were sparks flying, and they weren't just coming from you. I was an eyewitness, remember?"

She shrugged and changed the subject. "Time to load up for your appointment."

Thirty minutes later, she flipped through a magazine while Taggert played in the toy area at the doctor's office. Her sister had already gone back to an exam room. He flopped down in the chair beside her. "What's up, buddy?"

He wore a concerned expression upon his face. "Do you think the babies are behaving?"

She put a reassuring hand on his leg. "Your mom's been resting. We've both made sure she does. So, I think they are."

He shook off his melancholy. "Okay."

His moods were like the changing weather. This visit to help out was getting her better acquainted with her nephew. Which reminded her of her own biological clock ticking. "I'll make a deal with you."

"What's that mean?"

She searched for an easy explanation. "If you

behave, and the babies have a good appointment, I'll take you to see Santa Claus."

He jumped to his feet. "Yippee."

She chuckled at his enthusiasm. "Do we have a deal?"

He flashed a huge toothless grin. "Yup."

Two read articles later, Maggie emerged into the lobby. She smiled and held up two thumbs-up.

Relief spread through her body at her gesture. "What's the report?"

"I need to continue to rest and take things easy, but my labs were better than last week."

A sigh escaped, and the tension in her chest diminished. The concern she experienced since she'd received Jim's call eased.

"Were the babies good?"

Maggie smiled at his question. "Yes."

He jumped in the air and shouted. "Yeah."

She frowned at his excitement.

Her gaze met her sisters. "I promised him I'd take him to see Santa if he and the twins behaved at your appointment."

A tentative hand rubbed her stomach as she smiled. "Well played."

"Thanks. I'm learning."

****

What had Madison been thinking? Christmas was under a week away and the mall resembled a madhouse. Even for a Wednesday morning. They left Maggie safely tucked in bed with her latest package of Oreos. She glanced at Taggert. He stood on his tiptoes straining to see the jolly fellow in the red suit.

"Are we almost there?"

"There are still five in front of you." She smiled at his palpable excitement. "What do you want for Christmas?"

"I want a lizard." He shrugged his little shoulders with disappointment evident in the movement. "But mom said no."

A shiver traveled down her spine. She agreed with Maggie regarding the reptile. "What are you going to ask Santa to bring you instead?"

His face lit back up. "Have you seen the new Spiderman Lego set on TV?"

She shook her head. "I'm not sure I have."

"It's cool. Do you think Santa would bring some?"

"Do you take good care of your Legos? You don't leave them out for your mom to step on, do you?"

He glanced down at his shoe and dragged the toe across the floor a few times. "One time I left my Batman Lego on the floor. I can't repeat the word Dad said."

Madison lifted her hand and covered her mouth as she choked back a laugh. "I'm sure your mom would appreciate you not repeating the word." A glance at the line proved they hadn't made any headway. This Santa was pretty chatty.

She took a moment to study the area. The storefronts were designed in a circle, and in the center of the buildings was a beautiful, enclosed courtyard with a glass dome overhead. A beam of sunlight broke through the clouds to shine on the greenery planted below. Ryder had done a wonderful job designing the beautiful buildings.

An image of Mr. Wilson, their high school science teacher, taking a drawing away from Ryder during class made her smile. He'd always been doodling and drawing when he needed to pay attention.

The smile slipped as she realized Ryder strolled toward her. Had her mind conjured him up? She shook her head and looked again. But he still was there sauntering toward her.

"Hi, Taggert. Madison."

"Hey, Ryder. I'm going to see Santa."

He placed a hand on Taggert's shoulder. "Have you been a good boy?"

He frowned and shrugged his shoulders. "I dunno."

He gave the boy another pat on his shoulder. "Well, I'm sure you don't have anything to worry about." His gaze caught hers. "How did Maggie's doctor appointment go this morning?"

His concern touched her. "The appointment was good. We left her at home with a snack and the remote in her hands. But between you and me, the house will be too quiet. She'll be napping in no time."

A chuckle emerged from his lips. "Probably a rest well deserved."

She glanced briefly at the line; only three more children in front of them. Her hand encompassed the area. "I love the layout and design of the mall. You did a wonderful job."

His gaze surveyed their surroundings before coming back to meet her own. "The buildings are my plans, and I would love to take the credit for the beautiful patio area, but the courtyard design is purely based on Pilar's talent."

Once again, envy flooded her mind. Pilar. Would the story ever be different? "I didn't realize Pilar worked at your firm."

He frowned and shook his head. "She doesn't. Her interior design office is in Denver. She gives us a helping hand every now and then."

"Oh. I hadn't realized she no longer lived in Cedar Bend. When you said she was in Denver yesterday, I believed she was away on business."

"No, she relocated to Denver a little over two years ago."

Her mind whirled and her heart stuttered. Were they not an item anymore?

"She's coming home for Christmas. Maybe we can all get together and do something since you will be in town."

Disappointment crawled down her spine. "Yeah, sure." Did her regret reside in her tone? "Hey. I could also invite Zoe. She'll be in town this week."

"Wow. I haven't seen Zoe since graduation. Classmates are crawling out of the woodwork."

"I guess it's a mini reunion for Christmas in Cedar Bend." A gasp escaped as a tug on her skirt loosened her zipper. Her waistband started to slip from her waist. Taggert. What had he done now? With a glance down, she glimpsed his fist clasped around her zipper. A shocked expression was on his face as he quickly let go of the fabric. She was about to expose herself to Santa and his happy helpful elves. And Ryder. Oh, there goes Taggert's good boy status for sure. Her packages and purse fell to the floor as she grabbed her wayward garment. The children's chatter waiting in line faded as panic seized her body. She stood frozen. Now she understood the fear a deer underwent when captured by the beams of headlights.

"Hey, breathe. The bathroom is to your right." His

warm breath caressed her ear as he whispered encouragement into it.

She shook her head as a few things registered in her foggy brain. One, she needed to find a refuge, and two, the feel of his arms about her waist rivaled the pleasant experience of being tangled in tinsel with him the day before. The first action to flee was surely the most important, but her traitorous feet remained planted as she soaked up his nearness.

"Taggert. Stay here. I'll be right back."

As Ryder's words registered, she twisted to meet Taggert's gaze. "Don't. Move. A. Muscle."

Her nephew sighed and broke eye contact. "O…kay."

"Are you ready? Start toward the bathroom, and I will follow right behind you."

His body heat radiated against her back as she shuffled toward sanctuary. A sigh escaped as she eased the door open. She glanced over her shoulder and met his gaze. Still clenching her skirt, she backed away. Heat waves of embarrassment bounced off her cheeks. She opened her mouth, but the thank-you she intended to speak wouldn't emerge. At least when she puked on him, she'd been a little tipsy and didn't remember much of what happened. On this occasion, the memory would be embedded in her brain. Forever.

The restroom appeared empty. Her gaze encountered her mirrored image. Did she almost lose her skirt in the Santa line? Unbelievable. She shook her head to clear her thoughts before she twisted to examine where her skirt ripped. A quick inspection proved the fabric hadn't ripped, but…the zipper broke. *Great. Just great.*

Her musings were interrupted when a woman entered the bathroom and glanced her way. She hoped the smile she cast in the woman's direction didn't appear as a snarl. A peek down at her skirt proved her fairy godmother hadn't fixed her predicament in the few seconds she'd glanced away.

What was she going to do? Maggie wouldn't be able to help this time. Or Zoe. She hung her head in defeat. The only help was the man standing in the Santa line with her nephew. The day kept on giving.

"Are you okay?"

With a gasp, she spun to see the lady who'd entered earlier studying her with a critical eye. "Not really." Was the croaky reply her voice? She cleared her throat and pivoted on her heel to demonstrate her problem. "Unless you have a sewing machine or needle and thread in your small backpack, I'm pretty much out of luck."

The lady shrugged the pack off her shoulder. "Sorry. I left my sewing kit at home but let me see if I have a safety pin."

Euphoria bubbled within her chest. "Oh, please. I would appreciate any help you can give me."

After a few minutes of digging through the contents, she came up empty-handed. "I couldn't find any. Is there someone here with you who could help?"

A groan emerged from her lips. "Probably. I left my nephew in the Santa line with a friend from high school."

She swung her pack back upon her shoulder. "I could get your friend if you'd like. What is she wearing?"

A louder moan emerged. "The person is a he, not a

she." She leaned against the counter. "I've been nothing but a total spaz every time I get near him. This incident is another occurrence to go down in the books."

The woman laughed. "Old boyfriend?"

She shook her head. "No, worse. My high school crush."

The lady stuck out her hand. "I'm Amanda, by the way."

She shook her hand. "Hello, Amanda. I'm Madison." She grabbed her skirt and crossed to the door and peeked out. "Ryder is the gentleman standing in the brown leather jacket by the photo booth in Santa's village."

"I see him." She flashed a smile of reassurance toward her. "I'll get him for you."

"Thanks, Amanda."

A few minutes later a soft knock sounded on the door. "Madison?"

She opened the door wide enough to haul Ryder and Taggert inside the ladies' bathroom. Her hand smoothed out his jacket when she realized how firmly she held on. "Ryder, we have a problem. Or I have a small problem."

"Aunt Maddy. I'm sorry I 'bareassed you. Are you okay?"

Her gaze met Taggert's and she placed a hand on his shoulder. "I'm okay, bud, but my skirt isn't."

"I told Santa what I did."

Ah. Such a cute kid. When he isn't in trouble. She ruffled his already tumbled hair. "You didn't break my zipper on purpose. I'm sure Santa will understand."

"Really?" His whole body shook with the sigh of relief he exhaled.

The door opened behind them, and a lady gasped.

She hid a laugh behind her hand as she witnessed her stare at the sign on the door in confusion. "Is this the family restroom?"

Ryder scooted toward the door. "I apologize. Taggert and I were leaving." He grasped the handle and asked over his shoulder, "What do you need us to do?"

"The zipper on my skirt broke. I'll give you money for jeans, sweats...anything."

He took Taggert's hand in a firm grip and opened the door.

"Wait. I haven't given you money."

He shook his head. "Don't worry, we've got this."

She cast an apologetic smile toward the lady who still appeared a little confused. "My apologies. I experienced a slight wardrobe malfunction."

Instead of using the facilities, the woman opened the door and scurried away. *Great. Now I'm scaring away customers.*

A tap on the door a few minutes later indicated her rescuing knights were back. She opened the door to witness Taggert's hand still safely tucked into Ryder's. Someday he would make a great dad. Her gaze met his amused one.

He held up the bag. "Taggert picked them out. He said you would luv them."

Oh, boy. Could she handle any more of her nephew's love today? She dreaded what she would find inside the bag. A quick peek made her smile. Her nephew knew her pretty well.

Taggert smiled. "Do you like 'em?"

She patted him on his shoulder. "They are perfect. Let me see if they fit." Moments later she exited the restroom in her new Rudolph the Red-Nosed Reindeer leggings and smiled. They didn't exactly match her sweater, but she was happy to have the wardrobe crisis averted.

Chapter Eight

Ryder observed Madison giving Taggert a hug. He'd apologized again for breaking her skirt. Such a cute kid and his aunt, he smiled, was even cuter. His mind flashed back to the blue lacy underwear he'd glimpsed before she grabbed her wayward garment. If she realized where his mind had wandered when he held her in his arms, she'd retreat inside her shy shell.

His gaze took in her long legs encased in the leggings they purchased. He shook his head. Pilar wouldn't have put on what she wore. She'd draw the line at putting on pants with gaudy reindeer plastered on them. He'd bet she would have pouted and said they didn't match her sweater. But not only had Madison put them on, she seemed proud of her nephew's purchase. His gaze snared hers. "Everything better now?"

She laughed and drew a hand across her brow. "Whew. Crisis averted. Yes, everything is better now. Thank you for helping him find something for me to wear. What do I owe you?"

He could tell from the stubborn tilt of her chin she would pay him back and wouldn't take no for an answer. "How about you treat me to lunch before I go back to work?"

She nibbled her lower lip before she gave a quick nod. "I think we could arrange something. Where would you like to eat?"

"How about Chinese? There's a new restaurant down the street I haven't tried yet."

She took her nephew's hand. "Sounds good to me. Do they have a kid's menu?"

"Do they have chicky nuggets?"

He chuckled as both spoke at the same time. "I'm not sure about the nuggets, pal. But I'm sure they will have a hamburger if you're interested. Would you like to ride with me?"

She shook her head. "Car seat, remember? We'll follow you over there."

His cell rang as he unlocked his truck. He glanced at the phone. Pilar. He'd been avoiding her escalating calls. Her current agenda was asking him to relocate his company to Denver. Her current goal was for him to live closer to her and bigger contracts. He loved Cedar Bend and didn't want to leave. The expectations she'd placed on their relationship were clear. She wanted to get back together with the promise of a proposal in the near future.

As he drove into the restaurant's parking lot, he put his musings on the back burner. A glance in his rearview mirror showed Madison's car parking behind him. The idea of having lunch with her made him smile.

Madison's gaze met Ryder's as he held the door for them. His eyes twinkled with amusement. Did she want to know what had caused his secret merriment? Was he reliving the zipper incident? Why had she agreed to have lunch with him? Because she didn't want to miss the opportunity to spend time with him. She chose a table near the window. "Is this spot okay?"

He drew out a chair. "Perfect."

A server produced menus, and they took a few

minutes to scan the choices. "Taggert, they have some things on the kid's menu you would like. Do you want a hamburger and some mac and cheese?"

"They don't have chicky nuggets?"

She shook her head. "Afraid not this time, bud."

"Oh, okay."

She laughed at his obvious disappointment. "Well, try to contain your excitement." Ryder's laughter joined her own. Her nephew flashed a sheepish grin.

"What are you going to order?"

His question shook her from her musings. "I think I'm going to try the Mongolian beef with vegetables. You?"

"Why don't I order a chicken dish, and we can try a little of each other's entrées."

She smiled as she placed the menu on the table. "Sounds like an excellent plan."

After they placed their order, he leaned back in his chair and rested his hands on his stomach. "So, Madison Reynolds. Let's play catch up. You know what I'm doing. Tell me what you've been doing since graduation. Besides helping family out of course."

In high school, his direct gaze would have caused her to turn and run. She realized the anxiety wasn't present. Somewhere over the last few days, she'd become comfortable around him. Progress. "I attended the University of Colorado and studied finance. After graduation, I got a loan officer's position at a bank in Colorado Springs."

"Your degree and job don't surprise me." He smiled as he fiddled with the silverware in front of him. "You were always good with numbers."

His words took her aback. When had he taken

notice she liked to work with numbers? Before she could reply, the waitress placed their meals on the table.

"Can I try the white stuff?" Taggert pointed at Ryder's plate. "Is it good?"

"Sure." He took a scoop of his fried rice and put a small helping on his plate.

Her nephew wrinkled his nose before he flicked the pea peeking out from the rice with his fork.

She witnessed in horror as the green vegetable flew across the table and hit Ryder on his cheek. Her cheeks warmed with mortification. "Taggert."

"What?" He crossed his arms and sat back. "I don't like 'em."

"You can't hurl them at people because you don't like them. Tell Ryder you're sorry."

He peeked under his lashes. "Sorry, Ryder. Are you going to tell Santa?"

He picked up his napkin and wiped his face. "I'm sad to say he sees all this time of year, but I'll let him know you apologized."

His lip jutted out in a pout. "Okay."

"Hey. I found you. You weren't answering your phone."

Ryder smiled at the man standing by their table. "I was screening."

"I noticed."

He gestured to them. "Madison. Taggert. I would like for you to meet my business partner, Alex Fisher."

He extended his hand and shook both of theirs. "Good to meet you. Are you the classmate who is in town helping a relative?"

Taggert took a bite of his macaroni. "She's my aunt. She's helping Mommy."

Alex smiled. "And have you been a big help?"

He scrunched down in his chair. "Not today."

Madison smiled and ruffled his hair. "He's on sabbatical today. Which I'm not sure is good this close to Christmas."

Alex quirked a brow.

Ryder chuckled at her answer. "I'll explain later."

She indicated the seat next to Ryder. "Have you eaten? Do you want to join us?"

The invitation made him smile. "No, I haven't, and I'd be happy to. I'll order and be right back." A moment later he rejoined them. Before he sat down, he wiped something from the seat.

Ryder laughed at his actions. "Be careful, Taggert doesn't like peas. Don't get in his line of fire." He rubbed at his cheek. "He's a pretty good shot."

"Really?" He leaned across the table and whispered, "I don't like them either."

Taggert giggled before he took a bite of his hamburger.

Alex focused on Ryder. "Pilar called the office when you didn't answer your cell. She wanted to remind you she would be back in town tonight and is thrilled to have dinner with you. Though I'm not sure why she didn't leave a voice mail on your cell."

"Who's Piwar?" Taggert asked the question around a bite of food.

She patted him on the knee and whispered, "Don't talk with your mouth full."

He swallowed. "Well. Who is she?"

Ryder leaned forward. "She's a friend."

He tilted his head. "Another girlfriend? Like Aunt Maddy? How many can you have?"

She choked on the sip of tea she'd taken. "Taggert!"

"What?"

He cleared his throat, but before he could explain she interrupted. "Pilar is Ryder's girlfriend. They go on dates, eat out, and other activities."

"Oh." He glanced from her to Ryder. "You mean they do mushy stuff like Mom and Dad?"

Alex laughed at his friend's discomfort. "Thanks for inviting me to stay to eat. This conversation is pretty entertaining."

Ryder elbowed his friend. "Hush."

But her nephew wasn't finished with his questioning. "How come you don't want to do mushy stuff with Aunt Maddy?"

Heat flooded her cheeks. "Taggert. Time to go." She rose, signaled the waitress for the check and to-go boxes for their meals. "I'll pay like I promised." She boxed up their meals in record time and waved goodbye. She casually threw over her shoulder, "Nice meeting you, Alex," as she exited with Taggert's hand clenched firmly in her own.

Ryder stared after the duo as they left.

Alex cleared his throat. "Those leggings are such a fashion statement."

He chuckled and relayed the morning's events.

Alex snorted as he laughed and shook his head. "Poor Madison." He took a bite of his meal. "Why didn't you correct her when she said Pilar was your girlfriend?"

He frowned as he considered his question. "She didn't give me the time before she lit out of here."

He wiped his mouth and took a sip of his drink.

60

"You never answered Taggert's question."

His mind scrambled to remember what Taggert had asked. "What question?"

He wiggled his eyebrows. "Do you want to do mushy stuff with Madison?"

He leaned back, crossed his arms, and contemplated the question. His gaze met Alex's. "I may be in trouble."

Chapter Nine

Madison fiddled with the car seat harness as Taggert wiggled and stared. A frown marred his brow. "Sorry, Aunt Maddy. Did I 'bareass ya again?"

She paused in her actions and shook her head. His mispronunciation of the word was too accurate. "The word is embarrassed," she corrected. She finished with the belt and leaned back. It was hard to stay miffed at him when he gazed at you with his big blue eyes. "I think I've had enough excitement for the day. We will head home and check on your mom. Okay?"

He nodded and hugged his stuffed bear, his constant travel companion.

Thirty minutes later, Madison groaned. "Would you shut up already, what happened isn't funny!"

Maggie placed a hand upon her mouth to stop a laugh from emerging, but an unladylike snort emitted from her nose. "I'm sorry, Maddy, I know it isn't funny. I do." She took a deep breath, but a chuckle still tumbled from her lips. "I'm glad the incident happened to you and not to me. But I would have loved to be a fly on the wall and seen the whole incident."

"A pregnant fly on the wall, not inconspicuous at all." She studied her sister and the mirth radiating from her. "I'm glad I can provide such cheap entertainment. I could've climbed into a hole. The expression on Ryder's face, I won't forget anytime soon."

She paused mid-laugh and stared. After a moment of silence, she gripped her bulging stomach and burst out laughing again. In between the guffles, she busted out, "Oh, priceless."

Yeah. Priceless. "Maggie. You need to stop. All the jiggling can't be good for the babies."

As she wiped the tears from her cheeks, she waved a hand of dismissal. "Oh, posh. The doctor said my babies are doing wonderful."

"At the moment I'm worried about the mother."

"I'm in tip-top shape." She indicated her stomach. "Don't let this belly fool you. After all, round is a shape, right?"

A sigh of relief escaped her lips as she sat down on the bed. "I'm glad you are doing okay. Worry has plagued me since I received Jim's call last week."

"Everything will be okay."

A lump climbed into her throat. "I know." With a shake of her head, she shook off her worry. "Now." She rubbed her hands together and belted out her best interpretation of an evil chuckle. "My question is…how should I make my sister pay for her son's transgressions?"

A nervous expression crossed her face as she cringed. "Uh-oh, why do I have an awful feeling this will cost me?"

Madison tapped a finger on her lips. "For starters, I need to hit where it will hurt." With a snap of her fingers she exclaimed, "I got it! Oreos. There will be no more cookie runs until I am properly vindicated."

A horrified gasp escaped her lips. "Not fair." She rubbed her hands over her belly again. "That's hitting below the belt." She waved a hand over her tummy.

"Well, if I could tell where the belt was supposed to reside in my condition."

With a shrug of her shoulders, she said, "I'm considering 'you've got to hit 'em where it hurts' as my new motto."

Her sister played with the hem of the sheet on the bed. "I'm not sure I want to ask, but what are your demands?"

"Don't worry, Mags." She gave her a reassuring pat on the hand. "I'm not going to go overboard. Jim is back from his conference tomorrow, right?" At her nod she continued, "Zoe is coming home for the holidays. I'd like to go to the tree lighting in the park. It's been far too long since we got to hang out."

"Maddy, if you want to go out, that's fine. We don't mean to hold you captive here. Jim will be back, and I'm sure I can talk him into ordering food from somewhere. I'm not sure I can stomach his burnt offerings."

Rising from the bed, she started toward the door. "I'll make you something special tonight. Why don't you take a nap? Taggert and I will watch a movie. I hope the activity will keep him out of trouble. For at least an hour."

"Maybe." A chuckle escaped as she snuggled down on her pillow. "Thank you." Before she exited the bedroom, her sister snickered again. "By the way, I love your leggings."

With hands beside her side, she imitated a curtsy. "Why, thank you. What can I say? Your son has good taste in clothing."

Taggert was sprawled on the living room floor with his Legos as she strode by. "I need to make a phone call. Are you doing okay?"

His concentration didn't waver from his building project. "Yep."

Zoe answered on the second ring.

In a nasal voice Madison said, "Yes, ma'am, my name is Peggy and I'm taking a survey. Could I have a moment of your time?"

A chill entered her friend's voice. "I'm sorry. But no."

She laughed and yelled, "Wait, Zoe! It's me, Madison. Don't hang up."

A few seconds passed before her friend asked in a hesitant voice, "Madison?"

"Yeah. It's me."

Her friend snorted. "You almost had a dial tone in your ear. What phone are you calling from? I didn't recognize the number."

A chuckle escaped her lips. "Sorry. I couldn't resist. I'm calling from Maggie's landline. Are you still planning on coming home to Cedar Bend tomorrow?"

"Yes. I should be there around noon. Why?"

"Would you like to go to the town tree lighting tomorrow night with me? Maybe grab a bite to eat beforehand."

"Sure. I'll call you tomorrow to finalize the plans. Do you want me to call your cell?"

"Sounds good. Bye."

"Can I go with you to watch them light the tree?"

Little ears hear all. She'd forgotten he was near. His expectant gaze met hers. "Your dad will be back home tomorrow. I'm sure he will want to spend time with you. But we will ask. Okay?"

"Okay." His focus returned to his Lego skyscraper.

Chapter Ten

Ryder checked his phone for the third time in the last twenty minutes. Pilar was late. As usual. He'd agreed to meet for dinner. But he feared the agenda she had planned for the evening and over the holidays. He groaned and rubbed the back of his neck as he realized they dined in the restaurant they'd broken up in two years ago. Did she purposely suggest eating here?

He'd known she wanted to take the next step in their relationship, and he may have taken it if she hadn't forced him to make a decision right on the spot. Cedar Bend or her and Denver. Alex and his business had begun to pick up projects, and she wanted him to drop it all and move. With her. The discussion hadn't even happened before the ultimatum at the restaurant.

"Hi." Pilar leaned in to kiss his cheek before she slid in the booth's seat. "I apologize for being late. Mom and Dad were happy to see me and wanted to catch up before I met you."

"I can understand them wanting to visit. I haven't been here too long."

She studied him a moment before she leaned across the table. "You are looking well. I've missed you."

He leaned away from her advance. "It's good to see you too."

The waiter approached and refilled his water glass. "What would you like to drink, ma'am?"

Hiding a smile behind his hand, he watched her frown at the waiter's words. She hated to be called ma'am.

"An iced tea, please. With lemon." After they had placed their order, she studied him as she took a sip from her glass. "How have you been? Work going okay?"

"I'm good. Alex and I are ramping up to start building again in the new housing addition north of town in the New Year. With the holidays, business is a little slow, but I'm okay with it being not so time-consuming at the office. I think we were ready for a breather, especially since the mall was such a big project."

"If you lived in Denver, you would have endless possibilities of projects. There would be no slow periods. We could work together. You build the buildings, and I could decorate them."

He'd been expecting her words. A sigh escaped. "Pilar. We've had this conversation before. I'm happy here in Cedar Bend. I've made my life here."

"But you could make so much money in the Denver area and arena. Is it wrong of me to want the best for you? Besides, we can't continue this long-distance relationship. I want to get married. Don't you?"

Obviously, she'd blocked from her mind the fact they'd broken up. Several years ago. "Pilar, we haven't dated for two years. I've moved on. You need to as well. I don't think I'm your man."

She crossed her arms and huffed. "Who are you seeing?"

Her question produced images of Madison in his

mind. He shook his head. "That's not the point I'm trying to make. I love you, Pilar, but I'm not in love with you. I want you to find happiness."

Leaning forward she placed her hand upon his. "But I'm happy with you."

"I think you are comfortable with me. There's a difference."

Their meal arrived, and they ate in silence. She pouted, and he didn't know what else he could say to make her realize she needed to move on.

As they left the restaurant, Pilar put her arm through his. "What activity should we plan for tomorrow night?"

Had she always been this determined? Did he want to tell her what his plans were over the next couple of days? "Alex and I are going to the tree lighting in the park."

"Great. I could meet you there. What time are you going?"

He shook his head and gave her the time.

She waved a hand. "I'll see you tomorrow night."

He scrutinized her as she climbed into her sports car and drove away. The evening had gone almost exactly as he had expected. She wasn't taking no for an answer, and he didn't know what to do.

Small snow flurries began as he got into his truck. He sat a moment and stared out the windshield. Why couldn't Pilar see how happy he was? Had she always been this controlling? Without realizing the direction he drove, he found himself on the street where Madison's sister lived. He slowed as he noticed a lone figure in the front yard fighting with a blow-up Santa. He smiled and eased over to park alongside the curb.

Madison wanted to punch Santa in the face. The clerk had promised the directions were so easy even a child could do it. Obviously, she wasn't as smart as a two-year-old. She'd been outside messing with the ornament for at least thirty minutes.

"Could you use a hand? Or do you mind the jolly fellow in the red suit getting fresh?"

She rolled her eyes. Did he live for finding her in embarrassing situations? "I told him not on the first date, but as you can see, he has a mind of his own."

A deep chuckle rumbled behind her as a hand edged around her back to remove Santa's planted face from her own.

"Thanks." She eased back to survey the yard. "Everything else assembled like a dream. All except Mr. Santa here. He's being difficult."

"I'm surprised Taggert isn't out here helping you."

"Oh, he would be if he realized what I'm doing, but he is tucked into bed already. I plan on surprising him tomorrow." She finally glanced at him and as she studied him, she frowned. "Are you okay?"

He didn't have his usual ready grin. He shrugged instead.

Now she recognized something was wrong. Never in all the years she'd known him had she witnessed melancholy from him. She placed a hand on his arm. "Spill. You act like someone beat your dog."

His lips quirked a little. "I was the dog."

"Come on. Maggie has a porch swing. Let's sit and you can tell me what's bugging you." Two days ago, who would have guessed she'd be making conversation with the man by her side. She realized talking wasn't hard once she'd gotten over the butterfly-in-her-stomach effect. They sat in silence for a few minutes before she prompted him to talk. "So, are you going to tell me what has put the downtrodden expression upon your face?"

He shrugged his shoulders. "The problem I'm dealing with is something I need to work through. No need to depress both of us." His gaze met hers briefly before he stared out into the yard. "Santa's helper did a good job. The neighbors can't complain about your sister being a Grinch anymore."

She pondered the change of subject before she gazed at her handy work in the yard. "I think this elf deserves an extra cookie and some hot cocoa."

He chuckled and nodded in agreement. "At the least." He tilted his head and met her gaze. "Would the elf be interested in another decorating gig?"

"Maybe." She nibbled on her lower lip. "There aren't any blow-up ornaments involved, are there?"

The smile he extended reached his eyes this time, merriment twinkled from their brown depths. "I promise. You won't have any difficulties with assembly. I bought a tree yesterday for the office while I was at the lot. All Alex and I've had time for is to put the tree in the stand and add water so it wouldn't shrivel up. Would you and Taggert like to come and decorate our tree?"

Those dang butterflies took flight again in her stomach. She shifted on the swing. Just when she'd gotten them under control. He mentioned an activity where she'd see him again. "Do you have the ornaments already?"

"Yes. We rescued them from storage. We haven't taken the time to put them on the tree."

With a quick flick of her hand, she executed a jaunty salute. "Throw in some hot cocoa, and your elves will report for duty."

"Would Maggie be okay by herself if you visited the office tomorrow morning?"

As she considered what time to tell him she bit her lower lip. "I will double-check, but I think ten o'clock would be okay."

He plucked his phone from his pocket and consulted it a moment. "We have a meeting first thing in the morning, but we should be free by ten."

Stopping the movement of the swing, she rose. "Ten o'clock tomorrow." She retrieved her phone from her coat pocket. "Maybe I should get your number. In case we have to reschedule or call to cancel." Her fingers shook slightly as she typed in his number as he recited it. Ryder Sander's cell number was in her phone. She shook her head as she reminded herself it was just business.

A few minutes later, she waited as he eased his truck away from the curb. She frowned as once again she wondered about the reason he'd been down when he first arrived. He'd never told her the cause for his melancholy.

With a final disgusted scowl toward the blow-up Santa, she traipsed inside to get ready for bed.

Chapter Eleven

"Cool."

Madison laughed as Taggert checked out each yard decoration she'd assembled the night before.

"How late were you out here decorating?"

The chill in the air snaked down her spine, and she wrapped her coat a little tighter around herself before joining Maggie on the porch swing. "Everything assembled pretty easy except the guy in the red suit. He caused me some problems."

Her sister rested her head on her shoulder. "I know I sound like a broken record, but thank you." She indicated the yard with her hand. "Taggert, the tree, cooking, the cookie errands, and decorating." Her gaze met Maddy's as she smiled. "Are you sure I can't hire you full time? The pay is probably not up to your standards, but the benefit is you will be living close to your family again."

A wave of disappointment rolled over her. This time in Cedar Bend was fleeting. She'd enjoyed the last few days. More than she'd expected. A surge of homesickness she didn't realize she harbored overtook her. "My job is in Colorado Springs."

She patted her hand. "I know. You can't blame me for trying."

Taggert ran up the steps and halted on the porch. His breath puffed out. "What happened to Santa? He's all droopy."

A laugh escaped as she examined his expression. "I needed your assistance. Maybe before the day is over you can help me inflate him."

His chest puffed up with pride. "Sure."

"I have another mission for you to help me to complete."

A frown marred his brow. "What's a misson?"

"The word is mission." Reaching out, she combed a lock of hair from his eye. "Remember Ryder?"

"Your boyfriend?"

The thought of correcting him crossed her mind, but she didn't believe it would do any good. What she wouldn't give for his words to have a hint of truth. "Anyway, he stopped by last night and suggested since you are good at decorating trees, he asked if we could come by his office this morning and decorate their tree."

He jumped up and down. "Can we, Mom? Can I go?"

Maggie studied her a moment before answering him. "I think I will be all right for a bit by myself if you want to help Aunt Maddy decorate another tree."

"Wow. Two trees. Cool."

They watched as he rushed back out into the yard, scooped up a hand full of snow, and threw it in the air. "Is cool his favorite word?"

Her sister nodded and threw her a sly glance. "Showed up here last night, huh?"

The interrogation was about to begin if she didn't nip the conversation. "It's no big deal. Don't go getting all match-makerish on me."

Maggie rose from the swing and quirked an

eyebrow in her direction. "Are you making up words?"

"Maybe."

As she shuffled toward the door, she rubbed her protruding belly. "If you say so. I'm going back to my confined space. Thank you again for the yard decorations."

Pulling her cell from her pocket, she checked the time. "Taggert, I told Ryder we would be at his office around ten. We need to get some breakfast in your tummy. We've got a busy morning planned."

"Want me to make toast?"

The idea of him making cinnamon toast again made her stomach churn. "Why don't you leave the bread baking to me."

His shoulders lifted in a shrug. "Okay."

****

Ryder's phone vibrated in his pocket. He retrieved the cell to read the text. He smiled as he read Madison's message. She wouldn't arrive until a little after ten because convincing Taggert to brush his teeth had taken longer than she'd expected.

"What are you smiling about?"

His gaze swung to Alex's before he pointed to the tree in the corner, still unadorned of decorations. "I've called in reinforcements to decorate."

"I was beginning to enjoy the bare tree." He glanced at the tree and back. "Did you ask Pilar to do a foo foo design?"

At his words, he cringed. He hadn't considered Pilar's reaction to someone else decorating. How was she going to react? Her idea for their tree last year ran through his brain. "Uh. No. Madison and Taggert are going to come by to decorate."

Alex tilted his head and laughed. "Pilar will be pissed."

A tick started in his jaw. Yes, she would…if she found out.

"Good morning."

A cool breeze followed Madison and Taggert into the office. "You better have the hot chocolate you promised. My bones are chilled."

The cold weather had brought a rosy hue to her cheeks. He chuckled and pointed toward the Keurig machine. "Several different choices."

Before she took off her coat, she made her way to the machine to riffle through the packets. "Great. We will warm up and then get busy decorating."

Taggert bounded to his desk and jerked his stocking cap from his head. "Aunt Maddy decorated our yard. You should see it."

Static electricity from the cap made his hair stand on end. Ryder tried to smooth it down. "I've seen the decorations."

Behind his hand he whispered rather loudly, "Santa is dead. We got to fix him. She needs my help."

His gaze met her twinkling one. "I noticed."

"Good morning, Madison."

She tugged her gloves off her hands. "Hi, Alex."

"Ryder informs me you plan to help make our office feel like Christmas."

"I'll try our best." She chuckled and shook her head. "As long as there isn't a blow-up Santa, I should be able to help." A startled yelp escaped her as Taggert let out an excited squeal.

"Look, Aunt Maddy. They have a cat." He ran over to where a fat white cat lounged in a pet bed. Instead of being afraid of her nephew, the feline rolled to his back and presented his tummy for some scratches. "He likes me."

Ryder leaned forward in his chair and chuckled. "The cat is a girl, and her name is Snow. We found her last winter outside the building, shaking, and needing a helping hand."

Alex rose from behind his desk and joined them in the middle of the room. "I'm not sure who adopted who. Ryder and I take turns taking her home and making sure she's taken care of."

She chuckled as Snow climbed into her nephew's lap. "Well, she seems pretty content with her living conditions and the food rations." She shrugged out of her coat and handed it to Ryder's outstretched hand. "I know you'd like to play with Snow all morning Taggert, but we've got a job to do."

"Sorry, Snow, but I have to help Aunt Maddy." He rose once the cat settled back onto its bed and sighed. "I wish I had a cat. Do you think Mom would let me have one?"

The look she shot in his direction held a now-you've-done-it expression. "You will have to ask your mom." Her focus turned to the boxes in the corner. "Are those the decorations?"

His concentration wasn't on his computer, but on Madison and Taggert as they decorated. He gave up all pretense of working on the drawing and rose from his desk. They were unraveling lights when he offered to help.

Soon Alex joined, and they were all laughing when the bell above the door jingled.

"Well, how cozy. You know I would have helped if

you'd asked."

Pilar's icy words robbed the warmth from the fun moment. Ryder finished hanging the moose ornament. "Good morning, Pilar."

Her gaze scanned over Madison. "Madison Reynolds?"

She smiled and offered a hand. "Hi. It's been a while."

Her chilly gaze didn't ease as she ignored the outstretched hand. "Indeed."

Ryder rolled his shoulders to ease the sudden tension in them before he stepped forward. "What can I help you with?"

The wattage of her smile warmed. "Honey, I stopped to see if you wanted to eat out before we go to the tree-lighting ceremony tonight."

Honey? His gaze met Alex's. "Alex and I planned on eating at Tony's."

Her nose wrinkled in displeasure. "Really? Don't you want something other than barbecue? You seem addicted to the stuff."

Mentally he groaned. Why was she being difficult? "You can meet us at the park. Like we planned."

With an absentminded flick of her hand, she brushed her coat arm. "I guess. I'd hoped for more time together while I'm home." Her gaze flicked over Madison again. "How long are you in town?"

The question made his spine stiffen. Her inquiry bordered on rude. Before he could answer, Taggert sidled next to Madison and took her hand. "Aunt Maddy is helping me while Mom rests."

"Pilar, this is my nephew Taggert."

Ignoring Madison, she turned toward Ryder. "I can

help finish with the decorating." She approached the tree and frowned before she fingered an ornament with a bunch of bears rowing a canoe. "Really, Ryder. This is a place of business. Don't you think you should have a more professional appearance for your office?"

Alex placed the moose ornament he held on the tree. "These work for us."

She groaned, shifted, and unbuttoned her coat. "It's obvious you need professional help."

A frown crossed Madison's face before she retrieved her nephew's coat. "Taggert, we need to head home."

"Do we got to?"

Great. Pilar was running them off. Ryder picked up Taggert's stocking cap from his desk and held it out to Maddy.

Their gazes didn't meet as she took the cap and tugged it down on her nephew's head. "Your dad should be getting home soon. We can surprise him by having lunch ready."

He displayed his toothless grin and asked with eagerness, "Hot dogs?"

Ryder hid a smile as she cringed.

"Again? Don't you ever get tired of them?"

"Nope." He turned to hug Ryder's legs and glanced up. "Bye, Ryder. Thanks for letting us help."

"Sure, kiddo. Anytime."

"Oh. I forgot." Taggert ran over to Snow's bed. "Bye, Snow." He rubbed a hand over her head. "Be good."

Ryder felt disappointment as he observed Madison take Taggert's hand and open the door.

With a final peek over her shoulder, she said, "Bye

Ryder. Alex." She gave a quick glance to where Pilar stood in the corner. "Nice to see you, Pilar. Have a Merry Christmas."

Chapter Twelve

Madison had barely wrestled Taggert out of the car before he careened across the yard. "Daddy. You're home!"

The moment was a Kodak one. She smiled as he launched himself at his father. "Welcome home, Jim."

Jim hugged Taggert close and swung him around. "Hey, buddy. I hear you've been a big help."

"Yup. I was the man of the house."

"Great." He lowered him to the ground. "Run on inside and tell your mom you're back." He waited until he was inside before asking, "How have the last few days gone?"

The twinkle in his eye indicated he already knew how she handled his absence. "Maggie's already caught you up on events, hasn't she? Contrary to what my sister reported, keeping up with Taggert hasn't been too bad."

"I got a good laugh when Maggie told me about the zipper episode."

A visual of that day popped into her head and she cringed. "Yeah, well, the incident was only a slight setback."

His gaze slid to the yard. "You've been busy. Thank you."

The Santa still lay in a pile, but the other yard decorations were impressive. "I didn't want you getting reported by the neighborhood watch for being a Grinch."

"My neighbors understand my situation. But I'm sure they are glad you stepped in."

Taggert reappeared at the door. "Come quick. Grandma and Grandpa are on the phone."

Shrugging out of her coat, Maddy noticed Maggie nestled on the couch. She held the phone out and mouthed, "Don't tell on me." Jim took her coat as she grasped the cell. "Hi, Mom. Dad. How's the cruise?"

"Maddy. What a surprise to hear you were visiting. Weren't you planning on coming home for Christmas next week?"

Maggie's glare drilled into her back as she turned away from her stare. "Jim called me last week and told me he would be out of town for a conference and was worried about leaving Maggie by herself. So, I volunteered to come down early to give her a helping hand. Plus, you know how Jim worries. I'm killing two birds with one stone." A male snort sounded behind her. She silenced him with a wave of her hand.

"Honey. We can't talk long. We are in port for a brief amount of time and wanted to check on Maggie to see if she's doing okay. She says she's doing fine. Is she? Fine? Why else are you there? I know what you said, but we worry, you know. We should be there to help."

Turning, her gaze met Maggie's. "Mom. Take a breath. You're going to pass out if you're not careful."

A heavy sigh sounded over the phone. "Well, we worry. We planned this trip before we had knowledge of your sister's condition."

"Everything is fine. I wanted to help while you and

dad were out of town." They spoke a few more minutes before she ended the call.

Her sister let out a huge sigh of relief. "Whew. Thank you, Maddy, for not spilling the beans."

"Not saying anything was hard, you know. You better not let those babies come before they get back from their cruise or we will never live down the guilt trip."

A snort escaped Maggie's lips. "I hear ya. I'm taking things easy. How did decorating the tree with Ryder go?"

Moving a couch pillow aside, she sat down. "Fine."

Jim cleared his throat. "This sounds like girl talk. I'll make my exit and be in the kitchen wrestling something up for lunch."

An expression of panic crossed her sister's face. "Uh, Jim. Maddy will be in to help you shortly."

Her sister's attempt at derailing her husband from cooking made her smile. Poor Jim. He sure had a bad reputation.

Taggert plopped down on the floor next to them. "You should see Ryder's ornamts. He has bears, moose, and neat things to put on his tree. And he has a cat that lives at his work. Cool, huh?"

His mom smiled at his mispronunciation. "It's ornaments, buddy. I'm glad you had a fun time."

"Can I have a cat and animal ornamts to put on our tree?"

Maggie ruffled his hair. "Not at this time on the cat, but we can search for ornaments on sale after Christmas?"

"Cool." He jumped up. "Dad? Do you need my help? I can make the toast."

"So, spill. You're home earlier than I expected."

A sigh escaped and she shrugged her shoulders. "Nothing to tell. We came home early to make you and Jim some lunch."

"Bull." She shook her head. "You're biting your lip, so I know you're not being honest with me...or yourself."

Rising she began to pace. "We were having a great time until Pilar showed up." She frowned and waved a hand. "She hasn't changed one iota since high school. You'd think some of the snootiness would be knocked out of her by now, but no. The same ol' same ol'."

"Take a breath. You sound like mom when she gets on a roll."

Inhaling, she took a calming breath. "I don't see what a sweet guy like Ryder sees in her."

Maggie studied her a moment before a grin spread across her face. "You know, I don't think the feelings you have for Ryder is a crush. I believe you're in love with the guy."

Stopping mid-pace, she stared at Maggie. Love? "Now I know the pregnancy has messed with your head."

Her sister halted her words with a finger in the air. "Wait. Listen. This week I've seen you beam with happiness, and I feel Ryder created this change in you."

"Are you sure it's not the embarrassing situations he's found me in?"

She waved her words aside. "No. It's more. You're glowing."

The words stalled her denial. Was it possible the feelings she had were more than a lingering high school crush?

"Think about what I said. Don't brush off your emotions without studying how you feel."

The serious expression on her sister's face gave her pause. "I'll think about what you've said, but right now I'm calling Zoe to finalize our plans for this evening."

As she rubbed her tummy with one hand, she waved the other in dismissal. "Go. Make plans. But please don't leave Jim and Taggert alone in the kitchen for too long. I'm hungry, and if he cooks, the food may end up burnt."

Taggert giggled at his dad as she paused in the kitchen doorway. "I'll be right back. I need to make a phone call, and then I will be in to help."

Jim rejected her offer. "We've got this. Sandwiches are made, and we found a bag of Cheetos. No stove needed. So, both you and Maggie can quit worrying about me cooking with heat."

A wave of shame engulfed her. The poor guy tried. Not for the first time she wondered if her sister exaggerated about his cooking skills. "Well, thanks." She retrieved her cell from her purse and dialed Zoe's number. She answered after a couple of rings. "Hey. Have you arrived in town? Are you ready to make plans for this evening?"

"Sure." She paused. "You will never guess who I ran into at the gas station."

At her long pause, Maddy asked, "Are you going to leave me hanging with suspense?"

"Dustin."

As she searched her memory, she frowned. "The only Dustin I know was in high school. Dustin Keith."

"The one and only. I've invited him to join us tonight at the park."

"I haven't seen him in ages." She smiled at the memory of Dustin being her and Zoe's tagalong, like a third musketeer. "This visit is turning into a high school reunion."

"What do you mean?"

A recap of the week had Zoe laughing at Taggert's antics.

"What a pistol." She paused before asking slyly, "And how is your ol' crush, Ryder?"

Her mind rewound the conversation with Maggie from earlier and the mention of love. Could her sister be right? Were her feelings more than a silly old crush?

"Madison? You still there?"

Ignoring her question regarding him, she asked instead, "Where do we want to eat tonight?"

Her friend chuckled. "Okay. Conversation change. I get it. Subject closed. I'm game for about anything. You?"

"Hey, I will go anywhere as long as there isn't a hot dog on my plate."

"Let me guess. Your nephew's idea of the ideal meal?"

Madison tried not to groan. "You have no idea."

A chuckle sounded through the cell. "How about Tony's?"

This time she couldn't suppress the groan. "Anywhere but there."

"You like Tony's. Why not there?" Zoe sighed loudly. "Do I need to remind you, you said anywhere?"

"I know. I know. Sorry, but Tony's is where Ryder and Alex are going, and I'm sure Pilar will be with them. After this morning, I don't want to repeat the awkwardness this soon."

"Okay, I hear ya." A lengthy pause ensued on the other end of the line. "Have you eaten at the Italian place right off the square?"

"No. You?"

"Not yet. Let's give the new restaurant a try. What do you say?"

Madison's mouthed watered. "Sounds like a plan. What time do you want to meet?"

"How about five o'clock? Does the time work for you?"

"Sounds great. I'll meet you there."

"Okay. I'll let Dustin know the plan."

"See you in a while." She disconnected the call. The house was quiet as she exited the bedroom. A peek into Taggert's room showed him napping on his bed. She smiled and continued down the hall to Maggie's room. She raised her hand to knock but stopped when she observed Jim and Maggie snuggled together fast asleep. Retrieving a notepad from one of the kitchen drawers, she wrote her sister a note. *I've gone shopping and plan on meeting Zoe for dinner. We are going to the tree-lighting ceremony afterwards. Call me on my cell if you need anything.*

Chapter Thirteen

The delicious smells wafting in the air made Madison's stomach growl, reminding her the small sandwich she ate at lunch was hours ago. She studied the posted menu in the restaurant's foyer as she waited for Zoe and Dustin. Each item listed made her mouth water. She consulted the time on her phone.

The afternoon's shopping expedition had gone well. She'd finished all her Christmas shopping. Her reverie was interrupted by a squeal.

"Madison." Arms embraced her from behind.

She laughed as she pivoted and returned Zoe's enthusiastic embrace.

Zoe leaned back. "I hope you haven't been waiting too long. It took us forever to find a parking spot."

"With all the festivities this evening, I'm not surprised. It's good to see you."

"Hi, Madison."

The deep male voice had her turning with a ready greeting. Her smile slipped as she caught sight of the man standing off to the side. "Dustin?" Her gaze traveled from the top of his head to his feet. "Wow. You hit a growth spurt and then some." Gone was the short geeky awkward boy. The muscles defined on his well-toned body were impressive. "I wouldn't have recognized you."

"Can I get a hug?" He smiled and extended his

long arms.

"Sure." His muscles bunched as his arms wrapped around her. Wow. She eased back to glance at Zoe. Her friend mouthed, *hubba hubba*. She contained a laugh as they followed the hostess to an open table. Dustin scooted in after her to sit beside her in the booth.

"It's great running into you guys. I haven't seen you since graduation. Zoe caught me up on what she's doing at the store earlier. Where do you live these days, Madison?"

Was it her imagination, or did he sit in her personal space? She leaned back to meet his gaze. "I'm a loan officer in Colorado Springs. What do you do for a living?"

"I'm still here in Cedar Bend. I became a fireman."

Her gaze touched on his muscular arms again. His profession would explain his physique. She tilted her head. "Is being a firefighter what you wanted to do after graduation?"

A shrug made his arm muscles ripple. "I didn't know what I wanted to do. I stumbled upon the firefighter gig, but I'm happy with my career path."

Their empty plates sat in front of them as they sat and reminisced. They'd ordered a bottle of wine with their meal, and they all sat, relaxed, sipping wine and swapping stories from their younger days. Madison laughed at a story Zoe recounted.

Dustin's arm rested behind her on the booth cushion. He tapped her shoulder. "Hey. Do you remember the rainy day we attended band contest?"

A groan escaped as an image flashed in her mind. "Please. Let's not dredge up more embarrassing stories."

"Oh, no." He shook his head with vigor. "You've spent the last twenty minutes telling Dustin stories. It's only fair."

Zoe chuckled and reached across the table to place her hand over his. "But Dustin stories are so entertaining."

"Oh, no. Turnabout is fair play." His gaze met Maddy's. "You had bought a donut when the sky let loose with a downpour. Our sprint across the street was interrupted by you falling into a puddle."

A groan emerged as she hid her face with her hands. "I forgot you were there to witness me hydroplaning in the street."

A deep chuckle rumbled his chest. "Such a waste of a good donut. Only one bite out of the pastry before you let it fly."

"I know. I know. Don't remind me. I threw my donut at you when you offered to help me up." She paused and thought back to that day. "You know, I don't believe I ever thanked you properly."

His eyes twinkled and he shook his head. "Oh, no. It wasn't me who lent a hand to help you up."

"What are you talking about? Yes, it was."

"Your puddle jumping must have clouded your memory. You flung your donut at Ryder."

Huh? All these years she believed the gallant helper was Dustin. How could she have blocked Ryder from the memory?

Zoe laughed and leaned over the table. "You wore the jacket that absorbed the puddle like Bounty paper towels."

She smiled, but her mind still replayed the past scene in her mind.

Zoe snapped her fingers in front of her face. "Earth to Maddy. Hello."

"Uh. Sorry. I spaced out for a moment. What were you saying?"

Dustin shook his head. "I don't believe it."

What had she missed in the conversation? "What?"

"You're still crushing on Ryder, aren't you?"

"Did I hear my name?"

Shock rippled down her spine at his appearance. As her gaze met his, a wave of heat flooded her cheeks. Had he listened in on their conversation?

Zoe recovered first. "Madison was about to entertain Dustin with her Santa tale."

A chuckle emerged as Ryder shook his head. "There's an experience she won't forget anytime soon."

"What are you doing here?" At Zoe's gasp, Maddy realized how rude she sounded. "Sorry. My question sounded rude. What I meant to ask is why aren't you eating at Tony's?"

Alex joined Ryder by their table. "We were on our way there when someone changed our minds for us."

Madison's gaze collided with a frowning Pilar as she ambled up to stand by the men.

"I turned around and you both had disappeared." She reluctantly acknowledged them, "Hi, Madison. Zoe." Her gaze skimmed over Dustin, but she didn't greet him.

When she realized Pilar didn't recognize their former classmate, she contained her smile. "Ryder, Pilar, you remember Dustin Keith, don't you?"

Ryder extended a hand. "It's been awhile, Keith. How have you been?"

"Good. It's surprising we haven't run into each

other since we both still live in town."

Pilar's surprised gaze swung back to Dustin. Madison could understand her disbelief because she'd had the same reaction earlier in the evening. A dazzling smile lit up the other woman's face. "Dustin? Really? I didn't recognize you. You've changed a bit." Her gaze scanned over him again. "And I'd say all for the good."

He shifted uncomfortably in the booth.

The hostess cleared her throat behind the trio standing by their table. "Sir, your table is ready."

"Sorry. We got sidetracked." Before he followed the hostess away from the table he asked, "Are you planning on attending the tree lighting later?"

His question included all of them, but his gaze rested on her.

"That's our plan. We'll probably see you there."

Zoe leaned across the table once they departed. "Thanks a bunch, my friend, for introducing me to the hottie with Ryder."

"Oh. I forgot. The hunk is Alex Fisher, Ryder's business partner."

Crossing her arms across her chest she leaned back. "Now you tell me. We need to work on your manners."

Dustin cleared his throat. "Is it all right if I tag along with you to the park?"

Zoe and Maddy slipped out of the booth and laced their arms through his offered ones. "Sure. Lead on."

Ryder shifted in his chair to watch the threesome exit the restaurant. Was Madison dating Dustin? They'd seemed cozy, laughing, and joking with each other. He hadn't missed the other man's possessive arm draped across the back of her seat when he'd approached their booth. He shifted his gaze back to the menu before his companions caught him staring. Envy settled like a rock in his stomach.

"Ryder?" Pilar poked his arm. She frowned before asking sternly, "Did you hear a word I said?"

His gaze met Alex's amused one. "Sorry, I was studying the food choices."

Her brow furrowed deeper. "You've been acting strange lately."

He closed the menu and placed it on the table. "Have I?"

She flipped the napkin in front of her and placed it in her lap. "Yes, you have. What's up with you?"

Alex rescued him from the inquisition. "He's had a few projects at work he was trying to wrap up before the holiday."

"And I finished this afternoon, so now I can enjoy a few days off without a guilty conscience."

She scooted closer to his chair. "Great. I can't wait to spend more time together before I go back to Denver."

He mentally groaned. "What about your parents? Don't you want to spend time with your family?"

Her bottom lip jutted out. "I will, but I need to devote some time to you."

"Pilar." He nearly growled her name.

She sat back. "I know. You claim we broke up years ago. I'm not ready to give up on us."

Chapter Fourteen

Madison took a cleansing breath as she exited the restaurant. A chill had entered the air while they dined. "How about we go on foot the two blocks to the square. I'm sure we won't be able to find parking any closer to the park." She could use the night air to clear her head. Engrained in her mind was Pilar's possessive arm linked with Ryder's as they ambled away from their table.

They'd only taken a few steps when Dustin paused on the sidewalk. "Wait. You didn't share the Santa story."

Zoe chuckled and placed her arm around her waist. "Come on, Madison. Fill Dustin in on the fun you've had this week."

All three still laughed as they crossed to the next block. She paused in front of a storefront to admire a holiday display. Seconds later the smell of gingerbread floated on the evening air. She sniffed in appreciation. "Do you smell something delicious?"

Dustin and Zoe answered together. "Josie's Delights."

"I know we just ate, and I'm stuffed, but I vote we stop at Josie's and snatch a fresh gingerbread man."

Zoe exclaimed, "I'm right behind you."

"Me too."

Josie stood behind the counter as they entered the

bakery. She stopped arranging the display case and glanced up. "Doesn't this bring back memories? The three musketeers. I remember when you would stop by after school. I believe you kept me in business those first years I opened."

Madison laughed as she leaned in to look into the display case. "We did tend to eat our weight in sweets."

"What can I get for you?"

Her gaze met her friends' gazes. They all nodded and said at the same time, "Gingerbread men."

Dustin grinned and shrugged. "Or women."

Josie laughed as she slipped on a fresh pair of gloves. "Could smell them outside, I gather. I'm hoping to get a few folks in this evening with the tree lighting event going on tonight."

"Well, continue piping the smell of fresh-baked cookies outside, and you'll be swamped. I hope you have some help in the back. You're going to need it." Madison accepted her cookie and waited for Zoe and Dustin to pay for their own. "It's great to see you, Josie. I'll probably be back while I'm in town."

She waved from behind the counter. "Great. You guys have fun tonight."

Dustin teased, "At least it's not raining, Madison. We would hate for you to hydroplane and lose your cookie."

"Ha ha." She took a bite and closed her eyes. "Josie still has the baking skills, doesn't she?"

Zoe murmured her agreement. "Maybe we should stop by after we visit the square for another. Or a dozen."

She swallowed and nodded in agreement. "My nephew Taggert would love these." She finished her cookie while they waited for traffic to subside to cross the street. "Wow. There are probably over one hundred booths. This event is bigger than I remember."

They stopped at the first booth. The ladies behind the table sold wreaths. Zoe pointed to one hanging to the left. "Maddy. I see reindeer."

Dustin tilted his head. "Are you a reindeer fan?"

Zoe snorted and shoulder-bumped his arm. "Oh. She has a deer fetish."

With shock in his voice, Dustin asked, "How did I not know this?"

Madison ignored both as she retrieved her wallet to purchase the wreath. "Can I leave the wreath here and come back later when I'm ready to leave?" After she left her name with the lady at the booth, she faced Zoe. She pointed a finger at her friend. "Not a word. I know I have a problem."

Zoe zipped her lips with her fingers.

Dustin interrupted them. "Hey. I see someone I need to talk to. I'll be right back."

They both inspected his backside as he sauntered away. Zoe smiled and winked. "Who would have guessed nerdy Dustin Keith would turn into such a hunk, huh?"

She shook her head. "Not I."

"Speaking of." Her gaze met Maddy's. "What's the story with Ryder? We didn't get to talk since Dustin joined us for dinner."

She shrugged and bit her lower lip. "I don't have a clue."

Zoe frowned and shook her head. "You avoided the subject earlier with your subtle conversation change, but I'm not going to let you get away with dodging the subject this time."

Spotting a nearby bench, she took her friend's arm and led her over where they both sat down. "I don't know what to think. Ryder has helped deliver and decorate the tree I bought for Maggie. He stopped by the house when I was decorating the yard. He found Taggert and I in line for Santa. We've eaten Chinese food together, and he asked me to help decorate his office tree."

Zoe's mouth hung open a moment. "Wow. You've shared more activities in a few days than the whole time you attended high school with him."

"I know, right." She tucked her hair behind her ear. "I don't want to read anything into all these occurrences, but Maggie seems to think he's as into me as I am into him. But then there's Pilar."

She nodded in understanding. "The same old story. Pilar and Ryder, right?"

"Exactly." She nibbled on her lip. "Dustin is coming back. We need to shelve this conversation for later."

"Can I interest you ladies in some hot chocolate?" He pointed. "There's a booth down this way."

Madison searched the park while they waited in line for cocoa. She hoped she wasn't being too obvious on who she sought.

"Hey. I just remembered. We have an ugly sweater party tomorrow night at the fire station. Would you guys like to come?"

Zoe sighed and declined. "I can't. I have a family event tomorrow night, but I'm sure you can talk Maddy into it. If anyone has an ugly sweater to wear…Maddy would have one."

She bumped Zoe's arm. "Har, har, har. I don't consider my reindeer sweaters ugly."

Dustin laughed. "More reindeer. Now you must come, so I can see how crazy you are over the animal."

"What time does the party start?"

"Dinner is served at six. I'm on shift all day or I'd be happy to pick you up."

"It's fine. I'll drive myself and meet you there."

"Great. It's a date."

She inwardly cringed at Dustin's exuberance and the fact Ryder, Alex, and Pilar joined them. "Hi, guys. How was your meal?"

Alex rubbed his stomach. "I had the sampler, and I sampled way too much."

Everyone laughed, and the frown marring Ryder's brow eased. She wondered what caused his scowl to begin with. Her gaze slid to Pilar before landing on him again. Had they had a tiff over dinner?

Zoe nudged her in the ribs and muttered. "Stop it."

"What?"

"You're staring. Pilar's going to notice."

Hang Pilar, her mind screamed. She whispered from the side of her mouth, "I didn't think I was being obvious."

She patted her arm. "Only to me."

Dustin leaned down. "And maybe to me, because I know your secret."

She placed a hand on his arm. "Don't…"

He shushed her. "Don't worry, I won't let the cat out of the bag. But I'm not above adding fuel to the fire." He wiggled his eyebrows and swung an arm around her shoulder.

She giggled and pinched his muscular arm. "Flirt. I

bet you have plenty of ladies chasing you now. I'm sure the fireman's uniform helps, doesn't it?"

A blush bloomed on his cheeks.

Zoe took up residence on his other side. "Hey, were you part of the fireman's calendar shoot? My sister told me about the fundraiser when I was home at Thanksgiving. Madison and I like men in uniform. Maybe we will need to donate to a good cause."

If anything, his blush deepened, and a dimple appeared as he grinned shyly. "I'm July."

Madison nudged him. "Oh, did you pose with or without a shirt macho man?"

"Who's shirtless?" Pilar eased closer to join in the conversation.

Madison hooked a thumb over her shoulder in his direction. "Our friend Dustin here posed for the local fireman's calendar. He's Mr. July. We asked if he posed with or without his shirt."

Pilar's gaze roamed over his features again. "Well?"

Madison laughed as he squirmed under everyone's steady gazes. He mumbled something she didn't catch. She leaned in. "I'm sorry. We didn't hear you."

"Without."

The group laughed at his discomfort. Zoe chuckled. "I believe calendar sales just skyrocketed. Who wouldn't want to see this stud muffin without his shirt?"

"Hey, what are we? Chopped liver?" Alex crossed his arms and frowned.

Zoe's gaze roamed over him briefly. "Not exactly." She stuck out her hand and introduced herself, "I'm Zoe Pratt by the way."

He accepted her hand, and his frown eased. "A pleasure. I'm Ryder's business partner, Alex Fisher. Are you part of this high school reunion Ryder seems to have going on?"

"I am." She glanced about at the vendor booths in the park. "I'd be happy to show you the sights while we wait for the tree lighting."

"Sure. Lead on." He offered her his arm. "We'll catch back up with you guys in a bit."

Dustin offered his arm to Madison. "Care to take a stroll about the booths with me?"

Pilar stepped up and took his arm. "Actually, I'll go with you if you don't mind." She cast a glance in Ryder's direction. "Someone is being a bear tonight, and I could use some space from the black cloud."

Madison took a sip of her cocoa as they ambled away. She glanced back at Ryder. He did seem a little moody, but calling him a black cloud seemed a little harsh. "So, someone a little grumpy tonight?"

A sigh escaped him as the pair strode away. "I guess so." He glanced back. "And then there were two."

"Do you want to share what is making you irritable tonight?" She winked at him hoping to lighten the mood.

He shook his head. "I hadn't realized I was."

"The cocoa is good." She tilted her head toward the booth behind her. "Do you want to get a cup while we are here?"

"Sounds like a great idea." He paid for his drink before asking. "Was there a booth you wanted to see?"

"I've already purchased a wreath. I did spy a booth with ornaments I'd like to check out."

He waved his free hand. "Lead on."

"I'm hoping they have some animal ones like you have on your tree at the office. Taggert was impressed with your bears and moose." His deep chuckle sent a tremble down her spine. The sound should come with a warning label.

"A man with good taste and at such a young age. I'll help you pick out the best ones."

They found the booth she wanted moments later. The first ornament she spotted was a mama bear with two cubs beside her with pacifiers in their mouths. "Oh, isn't this one cute?"

He leaned in over her shoulder to examine what she held in her hands. "It's perfect. Do you think Maggie will have the babies before Christmas?"

His words scattered in her brain as she realized how close he stood. She frowned as she concentrated on what had he asked. Oh, yes. The babies. "Twins do tend to come early, but I've made sure she's taking it easier this week." She sighed. "I want everyone healthy." She caressed the ornament. "I've got to get this one for Maggie."

Not bothering to put any distance between them he leaned around her to pick up a reindeer wearing fake antlers. "Now I wonder who I know I could buy this one for?"

He stood close enough she could smell his woodsy cologne and see the crease of his dimple. Dimples. Another weakness she was finding she suffered from. "Taggert?"

His gaze met hers as he chuckled. "Oh. Taggert has a bigger reindeer fetish than his aunt?" He tugged his wallet from his back pocket. "This one reminds me of when you had the antlers stuck on your head."

Was Ryder Sanders buying her a reindeer?

"This one will go great with my other animals on my tree."

Nope. Her happy bubble popped. To hide her disappointment, she gazed at the other ornaments on display. She touched one with bears paddling a canoe. Taggert would love this one. Beside it were two raccoons hanging out by a trashcan. She grinned. Flynn and Mabel. After she made her purchases, she retrieved her phone from her pocket and checked the time. "They should be getting ready to light the tree soon. Should we locate the others and find a place to watch?"

As they weaved among the throng of people gathered in the park, she was aware of his firm hand on her lower back guiding them toward the tree. She glanced back to notice he seemed deep in thought and preoccupied. Pilar seemed correct in calling him moody. Had she ever seen him this quiet?

They caught up with everyone at the tree with only a few moments to spare. Pilar gave both an annoyed glare before focusing on the tree. Maddy didn't see why she was irritated at them. She was the one who took off on Dustin's arm instead of being with her boyfriend.

"Good evening, everyone. I'm Mayor John Clark. Welcome to the annual Cedar Bend tree lighting ceremony. I hope you are enjoying the Winter Festival. The booths will be set up all weekend. So, feel free to come back and support our local artists and business owners. Now, without further or long boring speeches, let us all count down from five to light this beautiful tree. Five. Four. Three. Two. One."

The crowd's oohs and aahs made her smile. The lights cast a pretty glow upon everyone. Her mood lifted as she observed the holiday spirit the gathering displayed.

Dustin turned and addressed all of them. "I hate to cut my evening short with everyone, but I need to swing by the fire station to help prepare for the party tomorrow."

At his words, Ryder perked up. "Is the station putting on a Christmas party?"

"We are hosting our first ever ugly sweater party." He glanced at them. "I've invited Madison, but everyone is more than welcome to come. The more the merrier."

Pilar snorted and looked away. "I don't own an ugly sweater."

A chuckle burst from Ryder's lips. "I'm sure all of my sweaters qualify as ugly. Count me in. What time does it start?"

"We start serving dinner at six. I'll see whoever is able to come tomorrow." He started backing away. "Thank you, Zoe and Madison, for inviting me along tonight. I've had fun."

Madison felt her phone vibrate in her pocket. She frowned when she read the screen. "I've got to get this. I'll be right back." She stepped a few feet away. "Maggie, is everything all right?"

A male voice chuckled. "Don't panic. It's Jim. She's not in labor."

Heart pounding, she placed a hand on her chest. "You scared the daylights out of me."

"Sorry." His voice held remorse.

With a slow inhale she took a deep calming breath. "Okay. What is the non-emergency?"

"I know you're probably enjoying yourself, and I

hate to bother you."

"But?"

"It's my fault." He groaned as if in pain. "I ate the last of the cookies."

A laugh burst from her lips. She covered her mouth to try to hold back her amusement, but she couldn't control her hilarity.

"Please say you will swing by the market on the way home and save me from the doghouse."

"You goof." She shook her head. "You don't own a dog. I'm near Josie's Delights. How about some fresh cookies?"

"Awesome! Can you get me a few of my own?"

His eagerness made her laugh. "I may be able to arrange something for you." Ending the call, she saw Ryder striding toward her.

His brow furrowed with concern. "Is everything all right?"

She smiled and nodded. "Everything's fine. Well, except for the fact Jim ate Maggie's last cookie."

A deep chuckle emerged from his lips. "Not the mistake he needs to make in his situation."

"Exactly. Jim called to beg for me to stop at the store on the way home. I told him I'd get some goodies from Josie's."

"You can't go wrong with any of her treats."

"I know. We already sampled her gingerbread men earlier. I'm sure Maggie won't be too unhappy if I grabbed some of those to bring home instead of Oreos."

"Mind if I go with you?"

As she glanced behind him, she didn't see his girlfriend. "Where's Pilar?"

He cast a peek over his shoulder. "She was behind

us visiting with Alex and Zoe."

Indecision made her bite her lip. She wanted him to accompany her, but she couldn't ask him to desert his girlfriend. "I can't ask you to leave your friends. Don't cut your evening short."

Zoe appeared at her side and hooked an arm through her own. "Do you need to go?"

"Jim called and wants me to make a cookie run."

"Great. We wanted to grab more of Josie's gingerbread men anyway. I'll go with you."

Pilar and Alex joined them as they said their goodbyes.

Alex quirked a brow. "Are you leaving us?"

"Sorry. You don't have to cut your evening short because we have to go. Enjoy yourselves."

Pilar hooked her arm around Ryder's waist. "We probably won't see you before Christmas. I hope you have a good holiday."

Her words grated down her spine. She excused them, like she used to do in high school. "You too, Pilar." Secretly she wished her words rang true. She hoped to dodge her presence the rest of her visit, but so far, she hadn't been so lucky. She waved to everyone before heading out of the park.

"Um. Was it my imagination, or did Pilar appear a little ruder than usual?"

They paused before crossing the street. Zoe's question rattled in her mind. "Ya think?"

She laughed and gave her waist an extra squeeze. "Okay, spare me your sarcasm."

Half an hour later, Madison let herself into her sister's house. "Honey, I'm home."

Maggie sat propped up on the couch. "Shh. Don't

wake up Taggert."

A gasp escaped, and she covered her mouth. "Sorry. I didn't realize the time."

"Did you have fun?"

She shrugged her shoulders. "Yes and no."

Maggie patted the couch cushion. "Plant yourself and explain. But first, pass me one of Josie's cookies I smell."

The events of the evening flowed out, and only when she paused, did she notice how tired Maggie appeared. "Okay. Enough chitchat. You need to go to bed."

A groan escaped as she rose slowly. "I won't argue with you. Night."

Fighting off a yawn, she deposited her uneaten cookie back in the bag and made her way to bed.

Chapter Fifteen

Madison awoke abruptly when an alarm sounded. She swung her legs out of bed and sprinted down the hall. A cloud of smoke wafted into the hallway from the kitchen. Entering the room, she spied Jim waving a towel under the detector with one hand and covering his mouth with the other. She rushed to the kitchen window and cranked it open. Silence reigned after a few moments.

Jim coughed and continued brandishing the towel about. "Sorry. I thought I could help."

The stories were true. She gaped at him in wonder. Maggie's tales about her husband being helpless as a cook were real. Up to this point, she hadn't believed her, but after the last few minutes, she was convinced. He sucked.

Taggert ran into the room. "What happened?"

She grabbed the skillet with cremated bacon off the stove. "Everything's fine. It was a small incident. Nothing we can't handle." She didn't know who she needed to try to assure, Taggert or herself.

Maggie coughed as she joined them. "Let me guess. Breakfast will be delayed?" She smiled before she shuffled over to Jim and leaned up to kiss his cheek. "I think I may get you cooking lessons for Christmas."

He wrapped his arms around his wife. "You may have found the perfect gift."

Tears pooled in her eyes as Taggert joined his mom and dad by hugging their legs. The tender scene, not the smoke, caused the waterworks. Not wanting to interrupt she backed from the room. "I'll go get dressed and go to the store. Besides bacon, is there anything else we need?"

"Oreos."

"You're going to turn into an Oreo if you're not careful. I think I'll buy you some carrots to offset your sugar intake." Maggie's muttering followed her from the kitchen as she left the room.

As she exited the house, she paused on the front porch. Disbelief trembled down her spine. "What are you doing?"

Ryder twisted away from the blow-up Santa. "I stopped by to fix your jolly fellow."

"Why?" She cringed as she realized she'd asked the question out loud.

He tilted his head and studied her a moment. "Because according to Taggert, he was dead and needed my help."

Even from the small distance that separated them, she could see his eyes twinkling with amusement. "No. I mean why do you feel like you have to fix Santa?"

He shrugged and ambled toward her. "I wanted to lend an extra set of hands. I know Jim just got back into town and this wasn't high on his priority list."

"No." She chuckled. "Burning breakfast ranks higher."

"Uh-oh."

Her keys jingled as she clicked the fob to unlock her car. "Yep. I'm going to the store as we speak."

"Mind if I accompany you?"

The keys nearly slipped out of her hands at his request. "It's a workday for you. Isn't it?"

"I won't tell the boss I'm playing hooky if you don't."

The image of Pilar's reaction of him spending time with her flashed in her mind. The other woman wouldn't like it. "I don't object if you want to tag along, but it's a quick trip for a few items."

Taking her pause in speech as permission, he opened the passenger door. "I call shotgun."

After she settled in the driver's seat, she shook her head. "Considering you're the only one going with me I think calling shotgun is silly."

A click echoed in the tiny confines indicating he'd buckled up. "Are you making smiley face pancakes?"

"Oh, I see. You're holding out for handouts."

"Busted." She maneuvered the car from the drive before he asked, "Do you have your sweater picked out for tonight's party?"

Her mind screamed not to ask, but when had she ever paid attention to her better sense. "Are you and Pilar going?"

"I'm not sure about Pilar, but the evening sounded fun."

Confusion rattled around in her mind as she chewed on her lower lip. He didn't know if his girlfriend would attend. Communication was lacking in their relationship. "It did. Sound entertaining anyway. I'd mentioned the party to Maggie last night before I got ready for bed, and she said she has several appropriate sweaters to choose from. She was happy to lend one to me. It's not like she will be wearing one anytime soon."

"Is Zoe going with you?"

She shook her head. "No. She has a family event tonight."

He peered out the side window briefly before his gaze swung back to meet hers. "Would you like for me to pick you up? We could ride together to the fire station."

No words emerged as she opened her mouth and closed it again.

"Madison?"

"Sounds like a plan." Did he notice how her voice cracked?

"Great. I could pick you up around five thirty."

All she could do was nod. She cast a sly glance in his direction. Would this be considered a date? But what about Pilar? She concentrated on parking the car at the store. "Yes. I'll be ready."

They were in and out of the store and back at Maggie's house in record time. She exited her car and tossed her keys into her purse. "Thank you for going to the store. I'll see you tonight."

He glanced at the house.

A giggle escaped. "Seriously you need to work on your poker face. Come on. I'll make you a pancake, but you need to get to work or Alex will send a search party for you."

"Yes." He pumped a celebrative fist into the air.

The smell of smoke still lingered as they entered the house. Taggert greeted them in the living room. "Hey, Ryder. Did you bring Snow with you?"

Madison frowned and glanced out the window.

He chuckled and ruffled her nephew's hair. "He means the cat. Right, bud?"

He nodded and smiled.

Ryder bent down. "Alex has her at the office."

Taggert swung his gaze up to meet hers. "Can we go visit Snow? Please."

"Not right now." She turned to make her way into the kitchen. "I need to make breakfast, and Ryder has put in a request for smiley face pancakes."

Taggert jumped into the air. "Cool." He took Ryder's hand and led him to the kitchen bar stools overlooking the stove area. "You can sit with me and watch Aunt Maddy make 'em."

"Wait just a minute." She placed her hands on her hips. "Am I the only one cooking here?"

Ryder placed a hand on Taggert's shoulder. "Aunt Maddy's right. I probably should help her with something."

He wrinkled his nose and sniffed the air. "Are you better than Dad?"

He laughed and shook his head. "We'll find out, won't we?" He shrugged out of his coat and dropped it across the back of the kitchen chair.

Opening a drawer, she pulled out an apron. "Are you as messy as my brother-in-law?"

He chuckled and settled the apron around his neck. "Maybe. What do you think? Does it work?"

Her laughter died in her throat as she noticed the adorned wording embellished across the front. *Bring the heat. Kiss the Cook.*

His gaze met hers before tilting downward to study the wording. He chuckled and caught her gaze. "Jim's?"

A nervous laugh emerged as an image of a sudden fantasy played in living color in her mind. Wouldn't she love to bring the heat? "Maybe? But knowing Maggie, I'm not one hundred percent certain it isn't hers." She retrieved a mixing bowl for the pancake batter. Her mind wandered back to kissing her assistant cook. What she wouldn't give to have that type of creative license. A wave of heat made its way into her cheeks. It's a good thing the smoke detector couldn't read her mind. Or it would be sounding again.

Not an hour later, Maggie groaned and laid down her fork. "Delicious meal. Thank you, Maddy and Ryder, for fixing an edible breakfast." She rose and picked up her dish.

"Uh-uh." Madison stood and stepped around the table to relieve her sister of her plate. "We've got this. Go back and put your feet up."

Maggie hid a yawn behind her hand. "Can I get this type of pampering after the babies arrive?"

Jim groaned, and his gaze landed on Madison. "Care to stay a little longer?"

"I've already told Maggie you probably couldn't afford me."

He shrugged his shoulders. "Can't blame a guy for trying."

Ryder rose and carried dishes to the sink. He looped the apron over his head, folded it, and laid it on the counter. "I hate to eat and run, but I need to get to the office. I'm surprised Alex hasn't called to check on me."

Rising, she carried dishes to the counter. "Is Alex joining us tonight at the party?"

"No. He had a previous engagement." He retrieved his coat from the kitchen chair and shrugged it on. "It was nice meeting you, Jim. Take care, Maggie and

Taggert."

Not ready for him to leave, she followed him from the room. "Did you remember to tell Taggert Santa is fixed?"

He stopped with his hand on the front door's latch. "I forgot."

"Okay. I'll tell him. Thanks for helping fix breakfast."

"No problem. I enjoyed the food and the company."

"I'll see you tonight."

He smiled as he opened the door. "Remember I'll be by around five thirty to pick you up."

"Okay." She closed the door behind him and crossed to the window to peek around the curtain to watch as he sauntered away.

"Enjoying the view?"

Busted again. She rolled her eyes and grinned. "Maybe."

Maggie laughed and shuffled toward her bedroom. "I don't blame you."

Chapter Sixteen

Madison regarded her image in the mirror attached to the bathroom door. She'd chosen to wear Maggie's ugly sweater with reindeer wearing sunglasses lined up singing Christmas carols. It wasn't the reindeer making the top ugly, but the fluorescent orange color. She'd paired the sweater with the leggings Taggert and Ryder bought to complete the ensemble. With a tilt of her head, she pondered the fact a week ago she wouldn't have imagined attending any type of function with Ryder Sanders. She mentally reminded herself the evening wasn't a date. He was being nice by offering her a ride. A corny smile emerged on her lips in her reflection. But a girl can dream…right?

Turning, she exited the bedroom and made her way down the hall to Maggie's room. A chuckle escaped as she observed her sister flip channels on the television. "By the disappointed frown on your face and the rate in which you are giving the remote a workout, I'm going to say you aren't finding anything worthwhile to watch."

With a flick of a finger, she muted the TV. "You would be correct. How can we have so many channels and not one worthy show to watch?" A chuckle escaped her lips as she stared at her outfit. "You look like you've arrived from the island of misfit clothing."

"Great. I've accomplished what I set out to do."

Her sister shook her head. "So much for impressing a man."

"What?" She drew a hand up and down to indicate the full length of her frame. "My curves aren't impressive enough?"

"You are such a goober. Have fun tonight. I want to hear all about the good times you're having in the outside world." She clicked the unmute button on the remote. "I'll channel surf."

"A self-pity party isn't going to help your mood."

"I know. Sorry. I feel so useless." At the sound of hammering from down the hall, Maggie chuckled, "But I'm happy to stay out of Jim's way while he finishes with the nursery."

A deep male curse floated down the hallway. They both busted out laughing at Taggert's reprimand. "Dad. Santa can hear you. You said a bad word." A low murmur followed her nephew's words. She hoped they were words of apology.

The sound of the doorbell ringing interrupted their laughter. Her heart rate tripped.

"Sounds like your date is here."

"It's not a date." She wiped her suddenly sweaty palms down her leggings.

Maggie shrugged and gave her a goofy grin. "If you say so."

The glare she shot at her sister didn't faze her. "I do." The bell pealed again as she passed by the nursery. Jim and Taggert sat in the middle of the floor with parts of the second crib laid out about them. "Don't get up guys. It's Ryder, I'm sure. I'll be back later."

Jim's "Have fun" echoed after her.

Ryder shifted his feet as he waited for someone to

answer the door. Did Dustin swing by and pick up Madison after all? Her car was parked in the drive. The deadlock clicked a few seconds later, and she swung the door open. A chuckle escaped as he took in her appearance. She was adorable in her reindeer sweater, leggings, and the deer antlers upon her head. If they had prizes tonight, he'd give her one.

The antlers jiggled as she tilted her head. "What?" She glanced down at her apparel. "Do I have food particles on my clothing I don't know about?"

Should he tell her how adorable she looked? He shook his head. "No. I wondered if you have something reindeer related for every occasion."

She smiled shyly. "Maybe." Turning, she said over her shoulder, "Let me grab my coat."

Ever since this morning when he'd helped her prepare breakfast, he'd been anticipating this evening. He considered tonight a date. Did she? Or was he just her offered ride to meet her old friend Dustin? He shook off his negativity as she appeared back at the door with her coat on. "Ready?"

"Your chariot awaits." He opened his pickup door for her and caught a tantalizing whiff of her cologne. For him or Dustin? This second-guessing was going to drive him bonkers. He needed to knock it off. After he started his vehicle, he adjusted the heat. "Have you seen the new fire station?"

"The station isn't on Maple anymore?"

He shook his head. "They built an updated building around the corner from the old one a couple of years ago. Pretty state of the art."

"Cool. I'll have to ask Dustin to give me a tour."

Me, not us. The single word answered his question

on whether she considered this evening a date with him. His jaw clenched. When he witnessed Dustin with his arm around Madison the night before at the restaurant, his mood had taken a nosedive. How did she feel about Dustin? Him? Was he considered only as a friend? Would he ever escape the friend zone? They arrived at the fire station in silence. "Here we are."

She focused on the building before turning her gaze to meet his. "You are right. It does appear state of the art. Impressive."

As they strode up the sidewalk, he nodded to other arrivals. The evening had a slight chill, but the snow they had experienced on previous days was currently at a halt. She shivered as he placed his hand at the small of her back. He leaned down to speak in her ear. "Cold?" Another shudder shimmied down her back. "Why don't you leave your coat on until you warm up?"

"Hey, guys. I'm glad you could make it." Dustin leaned down and gave Madison a hug and then shook Ryder's hand. "Let me take your coats and check out your ugly sweaters." He chuckled as she revealed her outfit. He shook his head. "Your sweater doesn't surprise me." He examined his sweater next. He shook his head and laughed as he read the shirt.

Ryder glanced down at the picture. Santa peeked out from an outhouse yelling at his reindeer, "I said the Schmidt house." He shrugged his shoulders. "My mom bought the top for me a couple of Christmases ago. I'm not sure it's seen the light of day until now."

"We've set up a few of our lockers as a temporary coat closet. Before you mingle, I want to give you a tour. I'll be right back after I hang your coats."

If the crowded room were any indication, the first annual ugly sweater contest could be called a success. A spicy aroma lingered in the air. Maddy's stomach growled. She hoped the chili tasted as good as it smelled. She glanced under her lashes at Ryder as he spoke with an older gentleman who had joined him.

The ride to the station wasn't what she expected. Something bugged him, and his silence was uncomfortable. Dustin rejoined her and interrupted her silent reverie.

He tilted his head toward Ryder and leaned down for only her to hear, "You're making progress. Are you here alone with Ryder?"

"Shhh." She glanced at him to make sure he hadn't caught his words.

Dustin bumped her shoulder. "Don't worry. I'm not going to spill the beans." He offered his arm. "Come on. Let me give you a tour. I'll show you where the calculated placing of the mistletoe can be found." He winked. "If you want to take advantage of the holiday sprig."

Her gaze met his amused one. She linked her arm through his. "Sounds devious, but you know I would probably never have the nerve to use the opportunity wisely."

As he patted her hand, he smiled. "I think I can help."

Twenty minutes later, she paused in a doorway. "I'm impressed. Cedar Bend has joined this century."

He nodded in agreement before he shifted closer and invaded her space.

"What...what are you doing?"

"Do you trust me?"

At her nod, he pointed a hand upwards. "I'm taking advantage of the mistletoe. You'd better put your heart into this. Ryder is watching."

A giggle burst from her lips as he grazed his lips across her own and dipped her low in a tight embrace. He righted her. "Now remember where the other holiday sprigs are located and give Ryder a good old-fashioned lip lock."

"Yes, sir." She gave him a jaunty salute. "Thank you for the tour. I will try to take advantage of the information you have given me."

"Did I miss the station tour?"

Her gaze met Ryder's. A deep frown marred his brow.

Dustin took a step back. "I need to help with the meal. Maddy can show you around. I'll catch up with you both later."

"Are you all right?" The scowl he'd worn when he joined them hadn't eased. "Did you have a bad conversation with the older gentleman you talked to?"

Dustin kissing Madison remained in his mind. He shook his head to try to erase the image. "Um, no. I guess you caught me deep in thought."

"While we wait to eat, would you like for me to give you a quick tour?"

"Sure." He followed, but his attention wasn't on what she pointed out. He couldn't shake the thought of the kiss he'd witnessed. Had she enjoyed the other man's embrace? It took a moment for him to realize she stood a few steps away from him studying him. Had she asked him a question?

She quirked a brow.

Yup, she'd asked him something and his mind had

wandered elsewhere. "I'm sorry. What did you ask?"

Her gaze shifted away from his. "Never mind."

Before she could turn, he caught her arm. His gaze shifted upwards to the sprig of mistletoe hanging above. Two can play this game. He eased his arms around her and draped them loosely about her waist. A slight tremble shook her body as her gaze tangled with his. Her eyes closed as he lowered his lips and brushed hers.

Behind them, a female gasped. "Oh. I'm so sorry."

The interruption couldn't have come at a worse time. He eased back and peered down into her eyes. He pivoted his head and glimpsed an older woman beating a hasty exit from the room.

"Why did you kiss me?" Her deep and husky voice echoed in the large room.

He pointed upward. "Opportunity knocked."

An expression of what looked like disappointment drifted across her face before she shifted and eased away from his embrace.

The light fragrance of her perfume tantalized his nose even as she took another step backwards. "Isn't kissing part of the tour? Dustin ended his tour this way."

She struggled a moment with righting the antlers on her head. "Well. Um. I think it's time we rejoined everyone else."

He splayed his hands. "After you." She led the way back to the kitchen area. He smiled at her distractedness. Score one for him. She hadn't seemed this flustered after her earlier kiss with Dustin.

****

The ribbon she'd won at the party for the most enthusiastically dressed wrinkled in her hand as she worked it with her nervous fingers. The silence on the ride to the party was nothing to the awkward quiet permeating the truck on the trip home. She scrambled her mind searching for a safe topic of discussion. He cleared his throat, and she glanced his way.

"Are we still going sledding at the hill tomorrow?"

Wow. She'd forgotten all about the plans she'd made with the others. The brief kiss he bestowed had left her shaken. "Yes." She rolled her eyes. *Come on. You were doing so well in the conversation department up to this point. Don't revert to your high school self.* She chuckled, "There isn't any way Taggert will let me change my mind, unless a blizzard occurs."

"I have noticed he can be persistent."

"You took the words right out of my mouth. This visit has shown me how much." Moments later he arrived in front of Maggie's house. He put the truck in park and shut off the engine. "You don't need to get out of the warm cab. I'll be fine to walk to the door by myself."

"Not happening." He shook his head. "My mother would not be happy if I told you to tuck and roll at the curb."

She laughed at the image in her mind of her jumping from the truck. "At least you stopped."

"True. One bonus point for me." He tugged on the door handle. "Wait there. I'll get your door."

The starlit night cast him in shadows as he made his way around the truck. Her heart sped up. Would he try for another kiss? The snow crunched under her boots as they hiked across the yard. The yard light shined upon his face, but she couldn't read his expression. "Thank you for going to the party with me.

I had a great time."

A smile appeared as he shifted closer and raised a hand to tuck a wisp of her hair behind her ear. "We got interrupted earlier."

Her breath caught in her chest as she struggled with his nearness. "There's no mistletoe." She scooted back against the front door as he advanced further.

A devilish twinkle appeared in his brown eyes. "Use your imagination."

As his lips settled on hers, she closed her eyes. This wasn't a brief brush like earlier, but a full committed lip lock. She sighed as he deepened the kiss. Any fantasy she'd dreamed up over the years paled in comparison to the reality of his actual kiss. The deer antlers upon her head slipped sideways as his hands cupped her head, further intensifying the kiss.

On unsteady legs, she leaned harder against the front door for support and looped an arm around his neck. His strong body followed. A tremble shook her body as he nibbled at her lower lip. A loud crash echoed nearby. Their lips parted at the interruption. His brown eyes sparkled with desire. She frowned as an odd feeling of being watched overtook her. Were the raccoons back already? She glanced toward the shadows on the side of the house as another crash sounded.

"Want me to check out the noise?"

His voice carried on a raspy whisper. She wasn't the only one who'd enjoyed the kiss. "It's probably Flynn and Mabel."

He eased away and frowned. "Flynn and Mabel?"

Her hands shook as she grasped the antlers and jerked them from her head. "The neighborhood raccoon bandits."

A low chuckle resonated from his chest. "No real threat then?"

"I don't think so."

He pivoted to go and glanced back before stepping off the porch. "Good night, Madison. I'll see you tomorrow."

Her lips still tingled from his kisses. She touched them in wonder. "Good night."

Chapter Seventeen

"Wake up, sleepyhead!"

Madison awoke with a jerk as Taggert jumped on the bed.

"Mom says you can't sleep the day away. You're burning daylight!"

She groaned and rolled over and put her pillow over her head. "Five more minutes, please."

"Mom said you would plead. Whatever that means. She told me to say, stop your whining and get up."

A peek from under her pillow proved he was still there. "I suppose you want some breakfast, right squirt?"

"Yep, my tummy is up and growling. We've been up for hours and hours waiting for you to get up."

"Goodness, you would have had to get up before the sun did."

"Nope. The sun was already peeking at me when I got up." He frowned in concentration. "Maybe it got up late this morning too."

Flinging the pillow aside, she rolled to the side of the bed. "I guess if we're going to eat, I had better get up, huh?"

"Yeah. Because we're going tubin' today."

There wasn't anything wrong with his memory. He remembered everything. "Are you ready for your first tubing trip?"

He tilted his head and smiled his toothy grin. "Can you make smiley face pancakes before we go?"

Mentally she groaned. "Don't you get tired of eating pancakes?"

He gave the mattress one final jump before he bounced off the bed. "Nope!"

Behind her hand, she covered a yawn. "Why don't we ask your mom what she wants for breakfast first?"

His little shoulders rose in a shrug. "I guess. If we have to." He headed out of the bedroom door and yelled, "Mom, you want smiley face pancakes, don't ya?"

Maggie's groan carried down the hall. With a shake of her head, she padded into the bathroom. A glance in the mirror showed her mussed hair and sleepy eyes. "Why, aren't you lovely this morning?"

As she emerged from the bathroom, the peal of her phone echoed through the house. Where had she left it?

"Hello."

Great. "Taggert, bring me my phone." She raced down the hall.

His giggle carried across the room as she spied him talking on her phone. "She's out of the potty now."

He handed her the mobile and took off toward his room. A male chuckle sent a shiver of awareness down her spine as she lifted the cell. "Hello?"

"Good morning, sleepyhead. I see your nephew has you on your toes bright and early."

A wince jarred her body. Out of all the people who could call, it was Ryder on the other end. Focus on something positive, she admonished herself. Like the kiss from last night. She cleared her morning froggy throat. "Yes. He's already trying to convince me to make smiley pancakes again this morning."

His deep chuckle carried across the connection. "I've got to admit the ones you served up yesterday were some of the best ones I've eaten."

The compliment warmed her heart. "Thank you, kind sir."

"Anytime." He cleared his throat. "I forgot to ask last night what time we are meeting this morning."

She glanced at the clock on the living room wall. "Let's shoot for ten."

"Okay. Want me to swing by and pick you and Taggert up?"

"Thank you for the offer, but I have Taggert's car seat in my vehicle already. We'll meet you at the hill. I'm picking up Zoe on the way."

"Alex asked if he could join us. I hope you don't mind him tagging along."

Zoe would be happy the handsome architect decided to join them. "Wow. Our outing is turning into a real party."

"Yes, it seems that way. I'll see you in a bit."

"Great. I'll text Dustin to let him know what time. We will see you there." She held the phone away from her ear and frowned. Had he groaned before he hung up?

"Madison, who were you talking to on the phone?"

She ambled down the hall to her sister's bedroom and leaned against the doorframe. "Ryder."

Maggie lifted an eyebrow in question before she smirked. "Should I ask if you had fun on your date last night?"

She straightened and strolled further into the room. Ignoring her question, she sat on the bed. "He called to ask what time we are going tubing this morning."

"Nice dodge." She fluffed her pillow and scooted further up. "Dish the juicy details. Because not only did you not answer my question, but you didn't bother to correct me when I said it was a date."

"Not much to tell."

"Hmmm. Then why are your cheeks so rosy?"

Maddy lifted her hands to cover her cheeks. "Why are you such a snoop?"

Her cackle could rival that of a hen. "You got a good night kiss, didn't you? How was the experience of finally kissing the man you've been crushing on for ages?"

A glance about proved Jim and Taggert didn't linger in the vicinity before she answered. "Absolutely wonderful, but brief. I swear I could flog your furry friends Flynn and Mabel. They interrupted my fantasy come true.

Her sister smirked.

"What?"

Her leer didn't ease. "Oh, nothing."

"Don't give me the load you're shoveling. The stare you shot in my direction meant something."

"Ryder has found his way into many of your plans this week. Did he initiate the kiss?"

Confused about the question, she confessed, "Yes, but I wouldn't make a big deal about it. Pilar is still in the picture. So, wipe those suspicious ideas from your overactive brain."

She tapped a finger against her lips. "I've never pictured Ryder as a player."

Where was Maggie going with this conversation? "What do you mean?"

She lifted her shoulders in a shrug. "I don't see him stringing several women along at a time. I think you don't know the whole situation."

Conflicted, she rose from the bed. "I don't know what to think. I'm going to fix breakfast now the inquisition is over."

"Blueberry muffins sound good."

"Are muffins a request?" She smiled as she teased. "I'll see if Jim will make you some."

"It's my demand, and don't let Jim touch them."

She saluted her. "Aye. Aye."

****

Zoe waved and eased into the passenger seat. "Good morning, Maddy. Taggert, are you excited for your first hill sledding expedition?"

"Yep. I'm primed and ready."

Zoe laughed at his words. "Let me guess. You got those words from your Aunt Maddy."

"Yep." He wrinkled his brow. "What do they mean?"

Maddy controlled a chuckle. "It means I wrestled you into clothes in a reasonable amount of time, and we are ready for adventure."

"Cool."

The parking area was full when they arrived. She glanced about. "Do you see an open spot?"

Both Zoe and Taggert craned their necks. "There. A car is leaving."

Her gaze followed Zoe's pointing finger. She punched the gas to get to the parking spot before someone else took it. A sigh of relief escaped her lips as she put the car in park. "We made it. Now, who's ready to go tubing?"

"Me!" Taggert yelled from the back seat with enthusiasm.

"Okay, kiddo. Let's get this fun started." She climbed from the car and helped her nephew from his seat. "First, we need to rent our tubes." He bounced from foot to foot in anticipation as they stood in line for the rentals.

Zoe leaned in. "So. How was the sweater party?"

Her cheeks heated. "I won the most enthusiastically dressed."

She eyed her with a suspicious glint. "The blush on your cheeks isn't from winning some award. Gimme details."

A glance down at her nephew proved he wasn't listening to their words. "One of my fantasies occurred last night."

A frown marred her brow. "Winning some ugly sweater competition was a fantasy of yours? How come I'm now hearing of this?"

"No. Not the contest, you goof." She leaned in and whispered, "Ryder kissed me."

"Oh." She winked and whispered. "And tell me was kissing him worth the wait?"

Her body trembled at the memory. "Oh. Yes."

"Can I have my own?"

Taggert's question interrupted their conversation. She leaned over and met his gaze. "Not this time. I think it would be safer for you to ride with an adult. I would hate for you to get hurt and give your mom something else to worry about."

A pout formed as his lower lip jutted out, but seconds later he nodded. "Okay."

"Hey, guys."

She returned a wave to Dustin as he strolled up. "Good morning. You made it."

"Yep. Parking was a hassle. They need a bigger place to park."

"Yes. We had a little bit of a problem as well."

He leaned over and stuck out a hand to Taggert. "And who do we have here? I'm Dustin."

He tilted his head as he gazed up at Dustin. "I'm Taggert. Are you a boyfriend of Aunt Maddy's?"

A grin spread across his face. "I am a boy."

Taggert looked down, shook his head, and mumbled, "Too many boyfriends."

Embarrassment traveled through her. She slipped her rental money to the clerk and spun Taggert around, directing him toward the hill. "Time to tube."

Zoe chuckled behind her as they treaded up the hill. "Your sister is going to have her hands full."

"You have no idea," she muttered.

At the top of the hill, she paused to catch her breath, and her gaze collided with Ryder's. He stood a few feet away. She expected to experience embarrassment after the embrace they'd shared the night before, but all she experienced was joy. "Hi." Her cheer slipped when she noticed Pilar also in attendance. "Good morning, Alex. Pilar." The other woman didn't return the greeting. She was decked out in a pink ski outfit. What she wore was appropriate for a black diamond run, not the hill at Cedar Bend. She glanced down at her scuffed hiking boots, jeans, and felt inadequate…again. Shoving her disappointment aside, she smiled at the trio. "You made it. Are you ready to get whipped by a four-year-old and his aunt?" Ryder's deep chuckle sent a pleasant shiver down her spine.

"Throwing down the gauntlet pretty early in the morning, aren't you?"

Alex put a hand to his chest. "Straight to the point and taking no prisoners. But I'm not worried."

"Oh, but you should be." She threw the tube to the ground and positioned it how she wanted. "Taggert, you will sit in front of me." He climbed on and she settled behind him. "The last one down has to buy the first round of hot chocolate." With a quick shove, they bounced off down the hill.

Her nephew's squeal of laughter made her smile. This morning's entertainment was for him. Not for her and her crazy fantasies. She leaned in to ask him, "Fun?"

"Cool."

The trip down didn't take long. He jumped up. "Again!" His eyes shined with the thrill of the ride.

"So, I'm guessing you didn't hate the experience."

"Nope. Do it again."

Zoe and Dustin bounded to a stop a few feet from them. "I'd forgotten how fun bouncing down this hill on a tube can be."

Zoe's words made her smile. "It's good to bring out your inner child to play every once in a while."

Taggert grabbed the rope and started dragging the tube back to the top. "Come on. You're burning daylight."

She shook her head. One of her sister's favorite sayings coming from his mouth sounded priceless.

Ryder slid to a stop nearby and called out, "Hey, your run was impressive."

At his compliment, her cheeks began to heat. "I told you I'm an expert."

"Yes, you did."

"I guess Pilar gets the privilege of buying the first round of cocoa." They both witnessed her bounce to a stop at the bottom of the hill. A spray of snow flew onto her face, and she sputtered.

Maddy tried not to smile. "She doesn't appear happy."

He shrugged off her comment. "Probably not. When she asked what I was doing this morning, careening down the hill on an inner tube isn't exactly what she had in mind. Plus, she wanted to ride down on the tube with me."

"A reasonable request since she's your girlfriend."

He opened his mouth to reply, but Taggert interrupted. "Come on, Aunt Maddy. I'm ready."

"The snow tubing bug has bitten. My sister will be so excited I introduced him to this." She puffed out a breath as she made it up the hill for the next run. "I'm so out of shape."

"Here, take my tube. I'll take Taggert down the hill while you catch your breath." Ryder placed his rope in her hands and sat behind Taggert. "Are you ready?"

"Yup."

"Then, let 'er rip."

A laugh bubbled out as she watched the duo bound down the hill. Their merriment trilled in the air at each bounce.

"I need you to stay away from my fiancé."

What? Fiancé? Had her ears deceived her? Madison met Pilar's heated gaze.

In irritation, she flipped a hand. "I dismissed the cozy tree decorating party at the office. The moment seemed harmless enough. But when my friend called me last night to tell me she witnessed Ryder kissing you at the fire station, I decided we need to talk."

Maddy opened her mouth to respond, but was instantly shushed.

"I don't want to hear your excuses. I caught you enjoying his kiss and wild embrace last night."

Wait. What? Her mind skittered back to the previous evening. She hadn't been at the fire station. If Pilar hadn't been at the party, she'd been at her sister's house. Spying on them. The rattling of the trash cans hadn't been Flynn and Mabel the neighborhood bandits. The culprit stood just a few feet away. "It was you. You knocked over the trash can."

"What if I did?" She yanked in frustration on her gloved hand before revealing a solitaire ring on her left hand. A smile of satisfaction spread across her lips. "We're engaged. So, I'm asking you politely to back off."

It took a herculean effort not to gape at the other woman. "Did you follow us from the fire station?"

"It wasn't hard. Neither one of you paid attention to what transpired around you." She shrugged. "When my friend called me to let me know about the hanky panky going on at the party, I decided to check out the situation for myself. Do you always make a habit of stealing someone else's man?"

If this conversation were Pilar's attempt at polite, she'd eat her old dirty boots. Ryder had initiated both kisses. Her words stung. Her chest constricted. She wasn't a heartless man stealer. The memory of the clanging trashcans again sounded in her mind. The feeling of being spied on wasn't from a bunch of scavenging raccoons, but a jealous fiancée. *Forgive me,*

Flynn and Mabel, for accusing you unjustly.

A sheen of tears formed, and she swung her gaze away from the other woman so she couldn't see them. What upset her more? The spying or the wonderful kiss reduced to nothing? What had Ryder hoped to gain? Was he throwing a bone to the girl from high school who couldn't shake the fascination with him? She searched for Zoe, hoping she stood near to rescue her from this conversation. A sigh escaped when she realized her friend flirted with Alex at the bottom of the hill. Help from Zoe wasn't going to happen soon.

"I know you've always had a thing for Ryder. Everyone noticed in high school, except maybe him."

Her jaw ached as she ground her teeth together. "We are just friends."

A sneer appeared on her face. "Friends with benefits?" She struggled to place the glove back on her hand. "You're seeing way too much of my fiancé for my comfort."

Bracing herself against any further words, she muttered, "Your concerns are noted." Swinging the tube down to the ground, she leapt upon it. With a thrust from her foot, she shoved off. The thrill of careening down the snow-packed hill had lost its luster. The tears she'd been holding back blurred the scenery as they fell. The freezing air caught the wetness and chilled her further.

Why had she been so stupid? She'd got caught up in the fact he spent time with her and let her guard down. Ryder was off-limits. Always had been. Always will be. Maybe now the fact would make it through her thick skull. She swiped a tear from her cheek. At her movement, the tube twisted and flew off the beaten path. Zoe yelled something but she couldn't make out her words. A moment later she realized she was on a collision course with an aspen. She braced herself as she bounced off the tree and pinged off another. A whoosh of air left her lungs as the tube settled to a stop. *That's going to leave a mark.*

Ryder scattered snow across her chest as he slid to his knees by the tube. "Are you okay?"

Taggert also dropped to his knees beside her. "You okay, Aunt Maddy?"

She lifted a hand to stroke Taggert's face but groaned at the shot of pain through her mid-section. "The verdict is still out."

Ryder's hands roamed over her arms. "Does it hurt here?"

A thrill raced through her body at his touch. With an awkward movement, she shoved his hands aside. "Give me a moment." She realized how rude she sounded and added. "Please."

Dustin settled on the other side of her. His fireman to the rescue face firmly in place. "Did you hit your head?"

"No."

"Where did you hit?"

As she tried to move, she grimaced. "My back mainly."

"Can you lean forward?" He poked around and when he put pressure on her ribs she sucked in a breath. "Okay." His gaze met hers. "A trip to the ER is in order."

"I can take her."

She waved Ryder's offer aside. "No. Dustin can get me there. He's the one with injury experience. Can

134

you and Zoe make sure Taggert gets home okay?"

Ryder nodded his agreement, but not before she'd seen an expression she couldn't identify cross his face. "Sure. No problem."

Dustin offered his hand and gently helped her stand.

Her gaze bounced off each of her friends gathered around. "I'm sure I will be fine. Sorry I crashed our party." This was Pilar's fault if she were to blame anyone. She stood a few feet away regarding her with a smirk on her face. Why did she let what she said or did bother her? She gave the group a final wave before putting a hand around Dustin's waist.

"Easy now. Let's not rush."

But she wanted to hurry. To get away from Pilar's knowing gaze and Ryder's concern.

****

Upon exiting the exam room, she noticed Dustin, Ryder, Alex, and Zoe all waited. "Did you get Taggert home safe and sound?"

Ryder stepped forward. "Yes. He's fine. He's worried about his aunt."

"I'm good. Nothing broken. My ribs are bruised."

Ryder breathed a noticeable sigh of relief.

"Whew." Alex smiled and wiped a hand across his brow. "I'm glad to hear it."

Dustin settled an arm around her shoulder. "Take it easy today. I don't want you hurting yourself worse. I would love to help you out this afternoon if you need it, but I got called into work. One of the guys has a sick child and couldn't make it in. I'll give you a call later to check on you."

Her gaze met his, and she gave his hand a pat.

"Thanks. I'm sure I'll be okay. I'll see you later. Thanks for coming out to tube with us this morning."

"Wouldn't have missed the thrill. Just like old times, huh? Well, except for you tackling a tree."

Zoe held up her keys. "I have your car. I'll drive you home."

"Thanks. I appreciate the ride." She glanced at Ryder and Alex. "I appreciate you coming by to check on me. You can be rest assured I will take it easy the rest of the day."

Ryder rocked back on his heels and stuck his hands in his back pockets. "You will let us know if you need anything."

She nodded as she shuffled toward the exit. "Will do."

Zoe waited until she settled in the car before the inquisition began. "Spill. What happened out there? I know your tubing skills. Losing control wasn't normal for you."

Once again, tears pooled in her eyes as she reviewed Pilar's words in her mind.

Her friend placed a hand on her arm. "Come on. I know something upset you. I'm not driving until you spill."

A chuckle left her lips. Same ol' Zoe. She could always depend on her. "Okay. I will tell you. But please drive. You're blocking traffic." She sighed once they left the hospital parking lot. "I will give you one guess who upset me."

Zoe's gaze met hers briefly before she focused back on the street. "Pilar?"

"Bingo. You got it in one."

An unladylike growl escaped her lips. "Want me to

go kick her ass? Would that help?"

"Yes."

Chapter Eighteen

Madison circled a word in her search puzzle and glanced out the living room window. Zoe dropped her off a few hours ago and she'd been on the sofa since, feeling sorry for herself.

What was her fascination with Ryder? The question churned in her brain over and over. Why couldn't she get all jittery with Dustin? He was a nice man, after all. But her body didn't react in the same way as when she was near Ryder. And now they'd shared a kiss...*Stop it!* She shook her head and focused on Jim and Taggert outside on the lawn. They put the finishing touches on the nativity scene she'd bought. Clouds had rolled in over the last hour and snow threatened. Jim hoped to get finished before the weather arrived.

She sighed and put down the puzzle book.

Maggie shuffled in moments later in her house slippers. "I caught the loud sigh from you all the way down the hall. What's going on? Other than the fact you got into a brawl with an aspen this morning." She sat down on the edge of the couch and eyed her.

A stab of pain shot through her mid-section as she shrugged her shoulders. Swift move, she mentally reprimanded herself.

"Come on. Keeping whatever emotions bottled up inside you isn't going to help matters any."

Suddenly, she wanted to cry. Her eyes filled with tears, and she tried hard to ward them off. She'd become a virtual watering pot today. "Sorry. You're the one who should be emotional, not me."

Maggie scooted closer. "Hey. It's all right. Taggert wasn't hurt this morning. I think your pride got bruised."

A hiccup escaped as she shook her head. "No. Careening into a tree isn't the problem."

Confusion appeared upon Maggie's features as she frowned. "Then what is the trouble? I guess I don't understand."

In frustration, she wiped the tears away from her cheeks. "Mostly, it's because I'm a goober."

"I won't argue with you there."

"Hey." She nudged her in the arm. "You're supposed to support me."

She drew her in close for a hug. "This better?"

A groan emerged. "It would be if my ribs weren't bruised."

"Oh, sorry." She leaned away. "If the problem isn't Taggert, then the problem is Ryder, isn't it?"

"Yes." Her breath hitched. "Pilar was there this morning. In a beautiful pink ski outfit made for a queen."

A bewildered expression appeared once again upon her face. "You're upset because of what Pilar wore to go tubing?"

"No. Silly. What she said and showed me while we were alone on top of the hill is making me bawl like a big baby."

"And what happened on the hill? I can't give my younger sister sage advice if I don't know what the crisis is."

Maddy sank back against the couch cushions. "She warned me to stay away from her fiancé as she showed me her engagement ring. I guess in case I didn't believe her, she showed props." She huffed. "And to add insult to injury, the sun peeked out from behind a cloud at the exact moment she showed me and the sparkle about blinded me."

Maggie eased back to lean against the couch arm. "I'm sorry. I think I would question her words and the jewelry."

"Why? What don't you believe? The ring on her finger?"

Her sister tapped her finger against her lips. "I'm calling foul. I think the little green jealousy bug bit Pilar, and she's grasping at straws."

Was her mouth hanging open? "Are you saying you think the ring was fake?"

"Maybe." She shrugged. "I think it's a little convenient the ring came out of hiding today. After you attended the fireman's party with Ryder last night, and he kissed the beejeebies out of you on our porch."

A choked laughed made its way up her throat. "There's the clincher. I accused your poor furry neighborhood raccoons for interrupting my best kiss ever."

"It wasn't Flynn and Mabel?"

"No. Pilar followed us from the party back to the house. She's the one who rattled the trashcan last night. I think she tripped on it."

Maggie sat in shock for a few seconds. "Wow. I'm stunned. Aren't her actions considered stalkerish?"

"Or like a jealous fiancée marking her territory?"

She shook her head. "They've been together forever. I'm surprised they aren't married already. I don't know what I thought spending time with him meant."

She tilted her head toward the tree in the corner. "The man who helped decorate our tree and fix breakfast didn't give me the impression of someone who is spoken for. I'm saying I think you need to dig a little deeper into this fiancée business."

"He's never denied Pilar is his girlfriend when the matter was mentioned in conversation."

"Did you give him a chance?"

Maddy frowned as she reflected on the last couple of days and the conversations. "I'm not sure."

Maggie rose from the couch and glanced out the window. "Well, I think I am. Why else would Ryder be walking up the drive talking to Jim and Taggert as we speak?"

"What?" She struggled to lean around her sister to gaze out the window.

"Don't get up. I'll let him in."

She swiped at her cheeks with her shirtsleeve trying to erase any lasting effects of her crying bout. Were her eyes all red and puffy? What did it matter anyway? She started to rise from the couch when he sauntered through the door.

"Hey. Don't get up."

Her gaze met his and she eased back down. "I won't argue with you. What are you doing here?" She cringed mentally. Did she always have to sound so rude?

He glanced at Maggie and then his gaze rested back on her. "I wanted to come by and see how the patients are doing."

Maggie choked back a laugh. "I'm good, and before she begins nagging me about being out of bed, I'm heading back there now."

He held up the bag he carried. "Before you go, I bought dinner for everyone. I wasn't sure if Madison would be up to cooking tonight."

Her sister's gaze settled on her. "Ryder, such a nice and considerate gesture. I'm surprised you don't have other plans this evening other than waiting on us invalids."

Maddy nodded in understanding to her sister's unspoken words. Her gaze implied not to be stupid. He's here with you and he's brought food. "What's in the bags?"

"Hamburger and fries."

Maggie sniffed the air. "Are they from Fred's?"

"Yes."

"Great. I accept."

Madison's stomach grumbled. "I agree. Thank you."

Around a french fry stuffed into her mouth, Maggie issued words of thanks and headed back to her bedroom.

"I also have a movie for us to watch while we eat."

At his words, she reflected back to what Maggie said. Is he acting like he is engaged? Did he feel sorry for her because she got hurt this morning?

The awkward silence that followed made him shift nervously from one foot to the other. "What? Do I have something on my face?"

"No." She couldn't make herself ask about Pilar. Instead, she indicated the couch and shifted, making room for him to sit. "Make yourself comfortable. What movie did you bring?"

"A classic."

"Does this masterpiece have a name? Are you going to make me watch a guy flick?"

He chuckled and showed her the DVD. "Do you like Goonies?"

"Oh, one of my favorites. There is nothing better than comfort food and a good flick. What else could I ask for?"

His brows wiggled up and down in a suggestive manner. "A little kissing on the couch?"

Unease shimmied down her back and she shifted away from his nearness. "Um, I don't think making out is such a good idea."

A frown appeared as he asked, "You don't?"

Before she could answer, Taggert rushed into the living room, his nose red from being outside in the cold. "Hi, Ryder. Whatcha doing?"

His gaze continued to study her a moment before he answered him. "I have dinner for everyone. I figured your Aunt Maddy wasn't up to cooking tonight."

"Cool."

"I also brought a movie to watch."

"Is it a cartoon?"

He opened the case and lifted the DVD out. "Sorry, squirt. No, it's not."

Disappointment radiated from his tiny frame. "Okay."

Jim shrugged out of his coat. "Let's wash your hands so you can eat, and then its bath time for you, buddy."

"Can I eat in here with Aunt Maddy and her boyfriend? I promise I won't make a mess."

Tears threatened again as she wished Taggert's words were true. But she would never be Ryder's girlfriend. It was time to quit living in a fantasy world. "Hey. Jim. Bring a towel back with you. We'll spread it out on the coffee table, and Taggert can have a picnic in here with us."

Her nephew skipped toward the bathroom. "Cool."

Jim trailed behind at a slower pace. "Thanks, Ryder, for bringing over dinner. For some reason, everyone is against me cooking."

In an attempt to lighten her mood, she leaned over and whispered, "You found out yesterday morning there's a good reason."

He chuckled and unwrapped his hamburger. "I'm glad I scored some points."

"Don't let it go to your head. They will turn on you on a dime."

His hand halted before he took a bite. "I would never have guessed your family as the vicious type."

"Okay. Maybe I exaggerate a little."

Taggert dropped down by the coffee table and placed a towel on the surface. "Whatcha bring?"

The bag rattled as he dove in with one hand and plucked out a hot dog and fries. "Will this work bud?"

"Great."

Jim reentered the room to claim his food. "If you don't mind, I'll eat back in the room with my wife. Are you sure Taggert is okay in here with you guys?"

Taggert eyed them in suspicion. "You aren't doing mushy stuff, are you?"

The bite of hamburger she'd just taken almost lodged in her throat and made her choke. She swallowed carefully before replying. "Uh, no. We're going to watch a movie."

He took a bite of his hot dog and talked around the mouthful. "Okay."

"I'll be back to put Taggert to bed."

"Oh, Dad. Can't I watch the movie with Aunt Maddy?"

"No. You can watch for a bit, but then you need to get ready for bed. You've had a full day and need rest."

A few minutes later, she chuckled as Taggert made himself comfortable on the floor, his hands propping his chin up and enthralled in the movie. The last few bites of his meal lay forgotten on the table. The classic movie was for all ages. A war nearly broke out when Jim came to collect him and tell him it was time for bed.

His lip jutted out. "But it's not finished."

Ryder leaned forward and tried to stem off a tantrum. "I own the movie. I'll let you borrow it."

"Okay." He slowly got up and gave her a hug before turning to Ryder and giving him one as well. "Night, Ryder. Night, Aunt Maddy."

"Goodnight, kiddo." Dread settled in her stomach. They were alone now. She stood up abruptly. "Want some popcorn?"

He leaned back against the couch cushion. "Sounds good."

As the popping of the corn stopped, she stared at the microwave. Her nephew had provided a buffer up to this point of the evening. The kiss from the previous night filtered through her mind. Would he try to kiss her again? Should she let him? Why was he here? Shouldn't he be with Pilar?

She jumped when she noticed Ryder standing in

the kitchen doorway. "You startled me."

He tilted his head and studied her for a few seconds. "Are you okay?"

"I'm a little sore."

A deep sigh sounded in the space between them as he shook his head. "You know I didn't mean your ribs. You'd been crying when I first arrived."

She ducked her head. "I'd hoped you wouldn't notice."

He crossed the room, tilted her chin up, and met her gaze. "I want to help if I can. Is it Maggie?"

Her gaze shifted to his lips.

A groan rattled in his throat before he leaned down to seal her lips with his own.

The heat from the night before hadn't been a fluke. She reluctantly broke free from the kiss and leaned her head against his chest. She inhaled deeply. His scent clung to his shirt heightening her senses, which made what she needed to say much harder to express. "We can only be friends."

To hear her whispered words, he dipped his head. "Sorry?"

She swallowed, met his gaze, and stated a little louder, "We can only be friends."

A disappointed expression crossed his features before he abruptly dropped his hands and stepped back. He glanced away and took a deep breath. "Sorry. I didn't mean to overstep." Without another word, he abandoned her in the kitchen.

Tears threatened again as he left the room. What had she done? Sealed her fate with the only person she'd ever loved is what. Yes. Love. She picked up the bowl of popcorn and rejoined him on the couch.

Ryder waited for her to settle before he started the movie. He could feel her gaze upon him, but he didn't want to talk. Something had happened between last night and this evening. He cast a sideways glimpse in her direction. Was he the cause of her tears? Without a word, she offered the bowl of popcorn. He took a handful and focused on the television.

As the credits ran, Madison's head dropped to rest on his shoulder. He peeked down to find her sound asleep. He took a moment to examine the smattering of freckles across her cheeks. With his index finger, he traced a few before dropping his hand. He'd wanted to ask her out in high school, but she'd been so shy. When he spotted her in the store the other night, all the feelings he'd suppressed in high school rose to the forefront. He'd hoped to start a relationship.

This evening she'd distanced herself both mentally and physically. She'd been acting strange since the tubing accident. He edged an arm around her shoulders and leaned his head back as she snuggled against him in her sleep. He stared at the lights twinkling on the Christmas tree for a few moments before he shut his eyes. The scent from her hair drifted up to tease his nose. The fragrance reminded him of summertime, light floral hints with a touch of sunshine. He smiled at his whimsicalness.

A throat clearing nearby woke him. He scraped a hand down his face and yawned. His gaze met Maggie's as she stood at the end of the couch. How long had he slept?

"Sorry. I didn't mean to wake you. I needed a glass of water. I assumed you'd left ages ago."

He shifted and eased away from Madison. She

didn't awaken. He stretched and grabbed the afghan off the back of the couch and covered her up. He smiled as she snuggled into the cushions and sighed. "Sorry. I must have fallen asleep."

Maggie studied him with a watchful gaze.

He held up a hand. "Before you say anything…I know I've worn out my welcome."

She shook her head. "No, you're fine. What are your feelings toward my sister?"

He paused in the process of putting on his coat to glance back at the sleeping woman. The soft glow from the lamp beside the couch cast shadows upon her face. "My intentions are good, but she told me tonight we can only be friends."

She crossed her arms over her burgeoning stomach. "Are you dating anyone else at the moment?"

He frowned as her question threw him. Didn't he say he had good intentions? Why ask? Did she not believe him?

She waved a hand. "Forget I asked. Thank you for bringing over dinner. It was delicious. I'll lock up behind you."

Still thinking over her question, he opened the door. "My pleasure. Good night, Maggie."

She shook her head and muttered something about clueless people. "Good night, Ryder."

Chapter Nineteen

Madison frowned as she tried to get comfortable. Why was her right foot cold? A shiver traveled down her spine. She shifted and groaned as her sore ribs protested. With a blink, she opened her eyes and startled backward when she encountered the quizzical stare of her nephew inches from her face.

"Whatcha sleeping out here for? Did you have a bad dream?"

In an attempt to shake the sleep fog from her brain, she shook her head. "No. I guess I fell asleep last night watching the movie." The afghan spread over her didn't cover her right foot. No wonder she'd been cold. She sat up, dragged a hand through her bangs, and glanced about. When had Ryder left? The aroma of his cologne still lingered. She tipped her head and whiffed. The scent permeated from her shirt. Had she cuddled him in her sleep?

Jim wandered in and hid a yawn behind his hand. "Taggert, you didn't wake up your aunt after I told you not to, did you?"

A guilty look crossed his face before he bolted to his feet. "Uh-uh. She opened her eyes all on her own."

Her brother-in-law grunted before he nodded. "Good. Do you want to help me with breakfast?"

He leaned in and whispered loudly. "Don't let Dad make pancakes. I like yours better."

"Why don't I come help?" She ruffled his hair and threw off the afghan. "You can be my cooking buddy."

"Cool."

Rising from the couch, she took a moment to fold the blanket. "Go ahead and get a bowl. I'll get my slippers and meet you in the kitchen in a minute." She smiled as he shot from the room. Her cell dinged as she searched for her footwear. The screen showed a text from Maggie. A chuckle escaped. Even though she was a few feet away, she'd used the power of technology to convey she did not want pancakes for breakfast.

Madison entered the kitchen to relay the bad news to Taggert. "You've been outvoted on the pancakes, bud."

"Oh, man." His head hung in defeat.

Feeling sorry for him, she patted his shoulder and whispered, "I'll make you one, but you have to help me make eggs and sausage for everyone else." Her phone dinged again. Man, her sister must have supersonic hearing. The text wasn't from Maggie, but from Ryder. Her pulse quickened.

—*Alex is taking Zoe by some of our house models today. Would you like to tag along? Asking purely as a friend, of course.*—

She paused over the message. Oh, right. Friends. She wished she could take the words back from the evening before. Would Pilar be going? She didn't know if she could take an up-close dose of the other woman this soon. *He can only be a friend. He can only be a friend.* The phrase reverberated through her brain a couple of times before she responded.

—*What time is this expedition to take place?*—

Only seconds later, he responded. He must have

waited for her reply. —*Alex is picking Zoe up a little after two. I could swing by and pick you up...if you like.*—

She hesitated. —*I need to check to make sure Maggie and Jim don't need my help for any reason this afternoon. I'll get back to you soon.*—

—*K*—

"Aunt Maddy. Are we going to start soon?"

"Sorry, bud. Someone asked me a question and I had to answer." She put the phone down. "Jim, Taggert and I have breakfast under control if you want to go entertain Maggie."

He swiped a hand across his brow. "Thank you. I hoped you would say that."

She chuckled and retrieved the breakfast items from the refrigerator.

A few minutes later, her phone binged again. She smiled at Maggie's message. —*Something smells wonderful.*— Before she replaced the cell back on the counter, it pinged again. This time her sister had sent a picture. Wondering if the text was a selfie, she grinned as she picked up her cell. The smile slipped as she regarded the picture. Ryder lay on the couch with her sleeping on his chest, his arms wrapped tight around her. His cheek rested on the top of her head and both of them were fast asleep and unaware of her sister's shenanigans.

—*What do you think of the picture I snapped last night?*—

She caressed the image. It was probably the only picture she'd ever have of them together. Instead of the snarky comment her sister expected, she typed, —*Thank you.*—

—*Don't let him get away. Ask him about his relationship with Pilar.*—

Obviously, Maggie still believed the other woman's actions were suspicious. —*I'll try.*—

Jim entered the kitchen. "I'm going to serve Maggie breakfast in bed."

Immediate concern flooded her mind. "Is she feeling okay?"

He waved her concern aside. "I'm spoiling her a little."

"Aunt Maddy, can we eat in front of the TV? That was fun."

A picture of syrup all over the furniture popped into her head. "Um, how about we eat at the table. Pancakes can get messy."

"O…kay. But I want to finish the movie."

"You can as soon as you eat your breakfast." She laughed ten minutes later as she washed her nephew's hands. "I believe you ate faster than I've ever seen you eat."

"Can I watch the movie now?"

At her nod, he rushed into the living room. "Do you need help turning it on?"

He stood in front of the TV. "I've got this."

She shook her head in wonder at his skills as moments later the movie played. "I'll be right back. I need to talk to your mom and dad."

"K."

Jim was propped up in bed with Maggie when she knocked on their door. "Is it okay if I go out for a few hours this afternoon? Or is there something you need my help with?"

She slapped her husband's hand away from the last

piece of sausage before answering. "We're good." Her gaze met Maddy's. "Are you taking care of the errand I texted you about?"

She shrugged and met her gaze. "Sort of. Ryder and Alex are going to show Zoe and I some of the new homes they've been building."

"Maddy, you don't have to ask permission every time you want to do something with your friends."

"I know. I wanted to make sure I wasn't needed before I took off."

Jim caressed Maggie's hand. "I go back to work tomorrow. I have a meeting in the morning I must attend, but then I'm off for Christmas vacation. Go have fun with your friends this afternoon. I'm here to keep an eye on things." He held up his hands. "I swear I won't cook, so you can rest easy."

A giggle escaped her lips. "Promise? I'll be back in time to help with the evening meal." She raised her cell and typed the message *expedition is on* to Ryder.

—*Okay. I will be by to pick you up in a bit.*—

The movie still played when she joined Taggert in the living room. She opened the closet to retrieve her coat.

He sat up from his reclining position. "Where ya goin?"

"Ryder is picking me up. He wants to show me something."

"Can I go?"

She patted his shoulder. "Not this time, squirt. Enjoy watching the movie Ryder left, and I will be home later to help make dinner."

He eased back down on his stomach with his chin in his palms. "Okay."

Chapter Twenty

Less than twenty minutes later, she observed Ryder's truck as he parked in front of the house. She called out a goodbye before she joined him outside. "Good morning."

Ryder pointed to the sky. "It's afternoon."

"So it is. Guess I didn't have enough morning caffeine."

Settled in the truck, he leaned back against the seat. He met her gaze, but still he didn't start the engine. "How are you feeling?"

A dull ache stole over her as she twisted to click her seatbelt. "Sore, but a lot better than yesterday."

"Glad to hear you feel better."

"I won't be hitting the slopes anytime soon, but when I'm back to one hundred percent I'll ask for a rematch. So, be prepared."

He smiled and winked. "I'll wait in anticipation for the challenge."

As he turned the key in the ignition and eased away from the curb, she studied him. "What time did you leave last night? I was out of it. I didn't hear you go." If she didn't know any better, she'd swear he was embarrassed.

A blush rose to his cheeks, and he cleared his throat. "Actually, I didn't leave until early this morning."

At his words, the blood drained from her face. Any other time she'd be happy to hear he'd spent the night, but if Pilar chose to do another stalk by, she was in trouble. She slumped down in the passenger seat trying to hide from any eyes that may be watching. How far would she take the next threat against her?

He shot a questioning glance in her direction. "Hey, are you okay? Did the bump I hit cause your ribs pain?"

He talked about a pothole, but her mind screamed she was headed for a sinkhole. "Um, no, I'm fine."

The look he aimed at her indicated he wasn't buying what she shoveled. She shook her head and decided not to focus on the Pilar the Psycho issue. "Where are we going this afternoon?"

He studied her a moment before he answered. "The housing addition we've been working on is south of town. A little past the strip mall where you visited Santa."

Once they left the city limits, she sat up straight and cast a casual glance behind them. She wouldn't put it past Pilar to follow them.

"You okay?"

"Sure." Had he noticed how fast she answered? "I was enjoying the scenery. I've missed Cedar Bend."

"Do you enjoy living in Colorado Springs?"

"Yes, but I sometimes miss my family and the smaller town atmosphere." She met his gaze. "How about you? Any plans of moving from Cedar Bend?"

"No." He shook his head. "My roots are firmly planted here."

She wanted to ask about Pilar and Denver, but he entered into the housing addition and she focused on the houses. "Are all these Alex and your designs?"

"Yes."

"Impressive."

His dimples flashed as he smiled. "Thank you."

"Which one are we touring?"

"My favorite actually. We are putting the finishing touches on it now. I've even contemplated making it my home."

At his declaration, she sat up straighter. What type of home would he enjoy? Zoe and Alex already stood in the drive of a beautiful mid-size cabin as they drove up. The home was different from its neighbors with a mixture of logs and brick. She understood why Ryder liked the house. "Hey, guys." They joined Zoe and Alex.

"Good afternoon. You feel better than yesterday?" Zoe's query and gaze held more than the voiced question.

Before she could answer, a car parked behind their vehicles in the drive. Pilar swung her hair as she exited the car.

Surprise, surprise, her mind screamed. She'd known in her bones they were being followed.

She sidled up beside Ryder and put her arm through his. "Imagine my surprise when I drove by and noticed you out here. What are you doing?"

Madison exchanged a glance with Zoe before returning her gaze to her gloved hands. Was she wearing the ring? Or was her sister correct in the assumption the ring had only been a prop yesterday?

Ryder unthreaded his arm from Pilar's. "Zoe and Madison were interested in seeing one of our latest projects."

She flashed a smile at them. "Can I come in? It's been a few weeks since I've seen the progress."

Although she included everyone in the question, her words and her Cheshire smile targeted Madison. Her intent was clear. *I'm a part of his life and you aren't.*

Ryder dragged a set of keys from his coat pocket. "I'm not sure much has changed since you were here last, but you are more than welcome to join us."

A hand stopped her from entering. She smiled at everyone. "I want a quick word with Madison, to see if she's all right after yesterday's accident.

The smile she presented was forced. Did anyone else notice? "You said everything you needed to yesterday." She turned to follow the others into the house.

Once again, she stalled her escape with a hand on her arm. "Obviously, not. He was with you last night."

Her body tensed as she readied herself for the onslaught of words she would endure. "He was nice enough to buy dinner and then we watched a movie."

Pilar's voice rose to a near shriek. "All night? That's right. I know he didn't leave until early this morning."

Zoe appeared at Maddy's elbow. "What's the hold-up? Maddy, you've got to see this kitchen."

A wave of relief swept through her as she followed her friend. She thrust Pilar's words aside as she glimpsed the inside of the home for the first time. "Oh, wow." A small foyer led into a grand room. But what caught her attention was the incredible river rock fireplace against the far wall. "This place is amazing."

Zoe grabbed her arm. "Wait until you see the

kitchen."

Ryder and Alex leaned against the counters deep in a conversation as they entered. They stopped their discussion and asked in unison, "What do you think?"

The light cherry wood cabinets and the marble countertops were gorgeous. A vision of Ryder standing in the kitchen with the Kiss the Cook apron rambled around in her head. She would love to see what they could cook up together in a kitchen like this one. Aware everyone's gaze rested on her, she shook the image aside. "What I've seen so far is beautiful. I commend you both."

Zoe grabbed her hand. "Let's check out the bedrooms." Once away from the others, she leaned in and asked, "What did Pilar want?"

An unladylike snort burst from her lips. "Besides Ryder? To warn me off...again."

Her friend opened her mouth to respond but paused as Pilar joined them. "Madison, will you be going home soon?"

Zoe tilted her chin, defiance in her gesture. "What is your problem?"

Her gaze remained steady on Maddy. "My problem, as you put it, is Madison swooping in and stealing my man. We all know she's been dying for the opportunity since high school."

"I don't have to listen to this." She tried to escape, but once again her firm grip detained her.

"He has cold feet." She poked a finger at her chest. "Leave him alone."

As she shoved her hand away, she noticed her gloves didn't cover her hands. Her left hand was bare. Hope flared in her chest. "Did you forget something today?"

A frown of confusion crossed her brow. "What are you talking about?"

She smiled and started to leave the room. "Never mind."

Zoe followed her. "Hey. Care to share what happened?"

"Did you not notice?" She glanced over her shoulder to make sure Pilar wasn't close behind. "She didn't have on an engagement ring."

"Hmm. Interesting."

"Indeed. I think I need to bring the subject up when Ryder takes me home."

Zoe nodded and muttered. "It's about time."

She smacked her friend's shoulder. "Hey."

"I'm saying I agree with your sister. You should have asked days ago."

She nibbled on her lip as she trailed behind Zoe. They finished exploring the other rooms in silence and met up with Ryder and Alex in the foyer. "What a treat. Thank you both for letting us tour one of your homes."

Alex smiled and extended an invitation. "Anytime you want to visit one of our designs when you're in town, let us know."

"I would love my own guided tour." She glanced about. "Did Pilar leave?"

Ryder twisted the lock on the door. "She left a few minutes ago."

Except when they stepped out on the porch, she made her way back up the sidewalk. "Ryder, can you help? My car doesn't want to start."

Maddy smelled a rat. Had she purposely sabotaged her car? Her mind scrambled with the notion even Pilar couldn't plan something so deceitful. Could she? But after the activities of the last few days, she couldn't discredit the notion. Her car was parked behind Ryder's truck, blocking him from leaving. He didn't have much of a choice in whether to help or not. She turned to him. "I can catch a ride with Alex and Zoe. I need to get home anyway."

Alex withdrew his keys from his pocket. "Sure. Zoe and I are going to a matinee." He glanced at his watch. "We have time to take you home first."

Ryder's gaze bore into her own. "Are you sure?"

Was he disappointed? "I am. Thank you again for showing us this lovely home."

He scratched his jaw. "We enjoyed showing you."

Seconds later, she sank into the back seat of Alex's car. As she peered out the window, she witnessed Pilar popping her hood and Ryder leaning in to examine the problem. What had she expected from this outing anyway? His confession of undying love? She snorted. Fat chance.

Chapter Twenty-One

Ryder stared at the engine under the hood of her car, but he wasn't focused on the task at hand. His mind replayed the scene from moments before. Madison climbed into the back seat of Alex's car without a wave or backward glance. All chances of anything other than a friendship vanished with her simple act. He contained his frustration toward Pilar. His hope of taking Madison out for an early meal and spend time with her derailed the minute she showed up.

"What do you think is wrong?"

Her words had his mind asking, *with this situation? Or with you spoiling my afternoon with Madison?* He leaned in to examine the parts. "You know I'm not a mechanic." His sideways glance caught her twirling a long piece of her hair. "Did it make any sound when you tried to start the engine?"

She shrugged and looked deep in thought. "Like what?"

He frowned and straightened. "Any noise? A click or nothing?"

Her lips tightened as she contemplated his questions. "I'm not sure."

The exasperation he'd suffered moments before bubbled over. He strolled to the driver's side of the car and opened the door.

"What are you doing?"

He eased down into the low-slung car and twisted the key in the ignition. The engine fired up with no prompting.

A nervous laugh escaped her mouth. "I promise it didn't start a few moments ago when I tried."

Could he believe her? Exiting the car, he shut the door and mentally counted to three. "Pilar. Why are you here?"

"What do you mean?"

His hands spread out to encompass their surroundings. "I know you weren't passing through the neighborhood. I spotted you following us after I picked Madison up from her sister's house."

Her chin tilted in defiance. "If you were aware of what I did, why didn't you call me on it when I showed up?"

He shrugged his shoulders. "Would it have done any good?"

She shook her head. "No, I suppose not."

A sigh escaped. "Pilar? What are you doing?"

"What do you mean?"

He wanted to groan. She asked the same question…again. "This week you've dogged my every move. Why?"

"I've missed you and wanted to spend some time with you. Is enjoying your company a crime?" She snaked her arms around his neck and leaned against his chest.

"In this case, yes." He disentangled himself and took a step back. As they stared silently at each other, his phone dinged. Retrieving the cell from his pocket, he read the text from Alex. *Dropped off Madison. Zoe has shared some interesting information regarding her friend. You need to shut Pilar down. NOW.* He frowned and turned the text around for her to read. "Care to explain what Alex is talking about?"

Her nostrils flared. "Everything was fine until she arrived home for a visit."

He crossed his arms across his chest and met her angry gaze. "We broke up two years ago. You didn't instigate this possessive stuff when I took out other women in town. Why do you have a problem now?"

"I'd hoped you would miss me, and we would reconcile." She stomped her foot. "The other women you dated didn't bother me. Madison does."

"What do you have against Madison?"

"Oh, come on. Why are men so oblivious? She had a crush on you before we even started dating in high school."

A ripple of shock jarred him. "Really?"

She rolled her eyes. "Clueless."

He skirted around the car and shut the hood. "I need to talk to her."

She deflated like a balloon. "You're in love with her, aren't you?"

He paused on the way to his truck and met her gaze. The events from the last few days and some forgotten ones from high school popped into his mind. He smiled as he opened the driver's door. "I guess I am."

Without another word, Pilar got in her car and drove away.

****

Ryder let loose a curse as another red light detained him. He tapped his thumb on the steering wheel. He should have asked Pilar specifics on what games she'd played this week before letting her drive off. How much damage had she wreaked? His mind played over the friend conversation Maddy had given him the night before. Another curse broke free. Pilar was the reason she cried the afternoon before, he would bet his next house sale on it.

The driver in the car beside him gave him an astonished gawk as he gunned the truck when the light changed to green. He eased off the accelerator. A speeding ticket isn't what he needed right before Christmas.

He parked in front of Maggie and Jim's house and smiled. The yard ornaments were completed, and the house appeared more festive than a few days ago. Taggert and his dad threw snowballs at each other in the front yard. The little boy's laughter echoed in the air and reached his ears as he exited his truck.

"Ya missed, Dad."

"I'm getting warmed up."

Taggert spotted him and ran over to greet him. "Hi, Ryder. Want to play snowballs with us?"

"Not this time, buddy. I need to talk to your Aunt Maddy."

The little boy shook his head. "You made her cry."

Huh? What did he do to upset her?

Jim crossed the yard and joined them. He placed a hand on Taggert's shoulder and told him to run inside, and they would continue the snowball fight some other time. They watched in silence as he trekked into the house.

"Madison is crying because of me?"

Jim shook his head. "She's upset, but Maggie is working on prying out of her why she's distraught."

"Can I talk to her?" Snow crunched under his boots as he started up the sidewalk.

After a few steps, Jim stopped him with a hand on his shoulder. "I think it would be best if you waited to talk to Maddy. I'm no expert on knowing when to butt out, but I think you need to give her some time."

He glanced back at the house. Damn Pilar. If she'd screwed up this relationship he wanted with Madison...with a frustrated groan he ran a hand through his hair. "Can you at least tell her I stopped by and I want to talk? It's important."

"I will."

Chapter Twenty-Two

Maggie replaced the curtain and shuffled over to the couch to sit beside her. "Ryder's leaving."

A deep sigh escaped. "I'm being stupid. I should have talked while he was here." She wrung her hands. "I got so irritated with Pilar…you know what happens when I get angry."

"You turn into the Hulk?"

She chuckled and wiped at her wet cheeks. "Almost. The madder I get, the harder I cry. My stupid emotions are out of whack."

Maggie snorted. "Don't talk to me about emotions. What do you think mine are going through these days?" She leaned back on the cushions and put her feet up on the coffee table. "You weren't able to have a serious conversation with him? I'd hoped you would clear up everything this afternoon."

"I was." She crossed her heart with her finger. "Honest. But she showed up. The damsel in distress trumps a serious conversation."

Taggert ran down the hall and into the room. "Feeling better, Aunt Maddy?"

She wiped her cheeks again with a tissue. "Sure, squirt."

"I told Ryder he made you cry."

His innocent words made her cringe. "You told him I was crying?"

He bobbed his head up and down.

Jim joined them as he stomped snow off his boots and stepped inside. "Ryder wants to talk to you. He said it's important."

Great. Between her brother-in-law and her nephew running interference, he probably believed she was a basket case. She frowned. What could be so important to discuss he needed to drop by? Was he finally going to tell her about his engagement? She glanced at the clock on the wall. Pilar's car problem hadn't taken long to fix. Had she finally convinced him not to hang out with her? Her imagination started running rampant on possible scenarios.

"Stop it."

She glanced at Maggie. "Stop what?"

"You are over psychoanalyzing everything. I can see it on your face."

A wave of guilt washed over her. "Maybe."

"Well, don't. Call the man." She rose awkwardly from the coach. "I'm going back to my mom cave and rest. Come along, Taggert. You can rest with Mommy."

"Ah, Mom. I'm not tired." Although he protested, he placed his hand in Maggie's.

Jim grabbed his cell from his pocket. "I'm making dinner tonight." Everyone groaned and he laughed. "Don't worry. I'm ordering pizza."

Left alone in the living room, she stared at the twinkling lights on the tree. How had this visit become so complicated? Her stay was to lend a helping hand for her family. Not fall in love and spoil a long-term relationship.

Her eyes grew heavy as the quietness of the house soothed her rattled mind. She snuggled down on the couch pillow and gave herself up to slumber.

****

Ryder checked his cell for possibly the one-hundredth time over the course of the last few hours. He wasn't sure what he expected, but not hearing a single word from Madison made him nervous. Reluctantly, he prepared for bed. Tomorrow he'd get a chance to talk, whether she wanted to or not. He couldn't let her leave town without her knowing his feelings.

Chapter Twenty-Three

A giggle jarred Madison awake. She blinked.

"You're finally awake. It's breakfast time."

Huh? She sat up and yawned. "It's morning?"

"Yup. We ate pizza without you."

How could she have slept so long? A glance outside confirmed a new day had dawned. Wow.

Maggie shuffled by with a hand on her back. "We saved a few slices of pizza for you if you want them for breakfast. I'm getting a small glass of milk and then heading back to bed."

"Are you okay?"

Her sister paused in the kitchen doorway. "Yeah. I'm a little tired this morning. I didn't sleep eleven hours like someone else in this house."

"Funny. Why didn't you wake me up?"

She snorted and stated, "We tried."

She rose from the couch. "I guess I needed the sleep." Collecting her cell from the end table, she checked for messages. A text from Ryder arrived around midnight. —*I'm coming over in the morning. We need to talk.*— Nervous butterflies erupted. Once again, he let her know they needed to talk. Was this a good or bad thing? "Taggert. Did your dad leave for work already?"

"Yup." He sat down on the couch, munching on pizza.

"Hey. Is that one of my pieces?"

He giggled before taking another bite. "Not now."

"Why, you little stinker." He dodged her as she made a grab for him.

He peeked around the couch. "Missed me."

"Madison."

She made a lunge for her nephew again.

"Maddy."

Her sister's voice penetrated their game play. Her gaze met Maggie's. She stood in the kitchen doorway, frozen with a glass in her hands.

"Madison, it's time."

She stumbled on a stray shoe on the floor. "What?"

Her sister gritted her teeth. "Pay attention. I said it's time."

Her hands shook as it dawned on her what she said. "The babies? But Jim's not here."

She rolled her eyes. "Duh. I need to call him."

Remain calm, she berated herself. "Taggert, go get your mom's phone."

Seconds later he raced back into the room. "Mom. Are you okay?"

Maggie took a couple of deep quick breaths before replying. "The babies are coming." She made a call and grimaced. "Voicemail. He must be in his meeting." Hanging up, she thumbed through the contact list. "I'll try calling Jan, his assistant." A sigh of relief escaped seconds later, "Jan. It's Maggie." She paused, listening to Jim's assistant for a moment. "I need you to get Jim out of the meeting and have him meet me at the hospital." Another pause. "Yes. Tell him I'm in labor. Thanks."

Madison grabbed her cell off the coffee table. "I'll

call Zoe. Maybe she can come watch Taggert." She dialed her friend's number. After only a few rings, her voicemail picked up. She hung up without leaving a message. What was she going to do? She nibbled on her lip as she stared at her phone.

"Maddy."

Her gaze swung from her cell to Maggie.

"We don't have time for you to ponder the situation."

A sensation of helplessness washed over her. "I wish Mom and Dad were back from their trip."

"Me too, but these two can't wait for their return."

A hysterical giggle bubbled from her lips. Seconds later, the doorbell rang. Who? Ryder. He'd planned on coming by to talk this morning. She ran to the door and wrenched it open. "Thank God." She grabbed his arm and hauled him inside. "Can you watch Taggert? Maggie's in labor."

His gaze swung from her to Maggie. "Wow." He ran a hand through his hair. "Go. Yeah, we're good."

She stood on her toes and kissed him quickly on the lips. "Thank you." She grabbed her sister's go-bag from the hall closet. "You ready?"

She chuckled and pointed downwards. "I don't know about you, but I think we both need shoes." Her gaze sought out Ryder's. "And I hoped my sister would be calmer than Jim. What was I thinking?"

Shoes on, she hustled her sister out to the car. Another contraction quaked through her as she settled into the passenger seat. "Oh, geez. Maggie, I'll hurry." The car was quiet except for her sister's labored breathing. "You're doing great. Keep it cool."

A strained chuckle escaped her sister. "Is the

reminder to remain calm a pep talk for me or yourself?"

"Both."

They shared a brief laugh before they arrived at the hospital. The staff rushed outside with a wheelchair. "Are you Maggie Clark? Your husband called and said you were on your way. How are you doing?"

"Just peachy."

****

Ryder shrugged out of his coat and draped it on a nearby chair. The morning took an unexpected turn. The speech he'd prepared in his head on the drive over was left unsaid. The quick kiss she'd given him gave him hope. His fantasy scattered as his gaze locked onto Taggert's. He could tell the little boy was scared. "Good morning, buddy."

"Hey."

He bent down on a knee until he was eye level with him. "Your mom will be fine." He flung his arms around his neck and hung on tight. He wrapped him in a hug. "Guess who I have with me in the truck."

He leaned back, anticipation obvious in his eyes. "Snow?"

"Yup. Do you want to help me bring her in?"

"Yes."

"Okay. Where are your shoes and your coat?"

He ran from the room and returned seconds later, dragging his coat behind him.

"Shoes?"

"Oh." He got down on all fours and crawled around the couch. "Got 'em."

He chuckled as he zipped his coat. "Quit squirming."

"Sorry."

Snow blinked at them as they opened the truck door. She stood up and stretched. A soft meow erupted as Taggert stroked her fur.

"Hi, Snow. Want to come play?"

He helped him bring in the cat. Once he had them settled on the living room floor, he made a call to Alex.

"Good morning. What's up?"

He cleared his throat. "A slight change of plans. I won't be in today."

"It's Christmas Eve. I can understand not coming into the office. I won't be here much longer myself."

"I have a favor to ask."

"What do you need?"

"I left the house with Snow and didn't bring any of her supplies with me. I'm at Madison's sister's house watching Taggert. Maggie went into labor, and they are on their way to the hospital. Can you bring by some food and litter? I'm not sure how long we will be here."

"Oh, wow. Sure. Text me the address."

"Thanks, buddy. I owe you one." He placed his phone in his pocket. Taggert sat cross-legged on the floor with Snow snuggled in his lap. "Have you had breakfast?"

Not taking his gaze from the cat, he answered, "Sort of. I ate Aunt Maddy's pizza."

He rolled up his sleeves. "How about I try making pancakes."

"Really?"

He smiled at his excitement. "I'm not sure they will be as cute or good as Aunt Maddy's, but I will give them a try." He retrieved the Kiss the Cook apron he'd worn the other day and searched the cabinets for supplies. Trying to get him to the table to eat the pancakes proved harder than the task itself. He didn't want to leave Snow alone.

When they sat at last at the table, Taggert eyed the pancakes.

The serious expression on the little boy's face made him pause with his fork halfway to his mouth. "What's the matter?"

"Do you think the babies will be born on Jesus's birthday?"

The way Maggie looked when they left, he wasn't sure she would make it to give birth on Christmas day. The babies would probably be born today. "We'll have to wait and see."

Finally, Taggert picked up his fork and began eating. Around a mouthful he announced, "Hey, these are good."

The statement was said with such amazement it made him chuckle. "I told you I could do it."

"When are you getting maryed?"

The bite he'd just taken stuck in his throat. He grasped his glass of milk and took a quick swallow. "What?"

"Maryed. To Piwar."

He leaned back in his chair. "Who said Pilar and I were getting married?"

"Aunt Maddy."

Dread skittered down his spine. "When did she tell you?"

He shrugged his small shoulders. "She told Mom after we went tubin'."

The events occurring on the day they spent on the hill replayed in his mind. Madison had her accident after she'd been alone with Pilar. "Do you know why she would think I'm getting married?"

"Piwar told her so." He took the last bite of pancake. "Can I go play with Snow now?"

He nodded absentmindedly. Anger like he hadn't experienced in some time washed over him. Could the damage Pilar caused this week be reversed? He closed his eyes and tilted his head heavenwards. Madison assumed he was engaged. To Pilar. The cold shoulder she'd given him was warranted. Who could blame her?

Chapter Twenty-Four

The peal of the doorbell jarred him from his musings. Alex had arrived with the cat supplies. But it wasn't his buddy at the front door. An older couple stood on the porch. They exchanged a shocked glance with each other before their focus swung back to land on him. "Hi. Can I help you?"

"Grandma. Grandpa." Taggert launched himself at the legs of the couple. "You're home." He leaned his head back and looked up. "Aunt Maddy's boyfriend is taking care of me. He brought Snow. The babies are coming."

Madison's mom leaned down and gave her grandson a hug. "You rattled off a lot of information, young man."

Her dad crossed his arms, quirked a brow, and looked him up and down. His scowl deepened as he read the apron. His gaze rose to meet his. "Boyfriend?"

He hadn't experienced the parental stare in years. It transported him back to his high school days. He cleared his throat. "Good morning, Mr. and Mrs. Reynolds. I don't know if you remember me, but I attended high school with Madison." He extended his hand to her dad. "I'm Ryder Sanders."

Her mom gasped and skipped over his introduction. "Did Taggert say Maggie's in labor?"

He cringed at the accusatory question. "Yes,

ma'am. Madison drove Maggie less than an hour ago." Someone would catch some flack, and he was glad it wasn't him. On this matter anyway.

Mr. Reynolds shuffled off the porch. "Come on, dear. We can drill the young man later about his boyfriend status with our youngest daughter. Let's get to the hospital."

She gave Taggert one more quick squeeze before stating, "See, I told you something wasn't right. Don't you ever give me a hard time about a woman's intuition again."

The banter continued down the sidewalk until the couple got into their vehicle.

Ryder glanced down as Taggert tugged on his pant leg.

"Grandma and Grandpa are mad at Mom, aren't they?"

He ruffled the little boy's hair. "Probably. But I think once they see the babies, they may forget their disappointment."

Back inside the house, Taggert climbed onto the couch next to Snow and started petting her. "Snow wants to watch a movie."

With a chuckle, he made his way to the shelf holding the DVDs. "What movie does Snow want to watch?"

"Yours."

He frowned trying to follow what he said. "You mean the one we watched the other night?"

"Yup."

****

Madison paced the waiting area. Jim arrived not long after they'd wheeled Maggie to the birthing center

177

at the hospital. She had to give him credit. His calm amazed her. His anxiety from a couple of days ago was gone. She sat down but then bounced back up again. The babies were early, but not unreasonably so. She hoped everyone was healthy.

She nibbled on a thumbnail. Should she check on how Ryder was doing with Taggert? They'd left in such haste this morning. A glance at the clock on the wall showed a little before noon. She dragged her phone from her back pocket. What would she say? Yesterday had ended on such an awkward note. Nerves made her pause.

"Madison Rea Reynolds, you are in deep trouble."

Jolted, she pivoted to stare at her parents standing in the waiting room doorway. Both wore an irritated scowl. "Um. You're not on the boat."

Her mother crossed her arms over her chest but didn't utter another word. She squirmed. Growing up it had only taken "the stare" to get both her and Maggie to talk. She believed she'd outgrown it, but she found words bubbling forth with little control. "Jim called me last week and said the doctor had put Maggie on bed rest. I asked off work, and I've been home helping take care of Taggert. It's Maggie's fault. She told me not to tell when I talked to you on the phone."

Her mom quirked a brow. The action a silent question if she'd shared everything she needed to know.

She shifted nervously as her mom continued the intimidating stare. "Then there is Ryder. He's the one I had a secret crush on in high school. We've been hanging out this week, but I think he's engaged to Pilar." She shook her head and bit her lower lip. "Actually, I'm not sure about the last part. I still need to clarify if it's true."

"Oh, you mean the young man wearing an apron requesting someone to bring the heat?" Her mother chuckled. "From the color in your cheeks, I'm assuming he accomplished the goal."

She waved her mother's words aside with a hand. "Well, nonetheless, I'm sorry we kept Maggie's house arrest from you, but you've been saving years for this trip and she didn't want you to worry. Or rush home." She frowned as she asked, "Which brings me to the question, why are you here? You weren't supposed to arrive back until next weekend."

Silent up to this point, her dad stepped forward. "Call it woman's intuition. That's the lecture I've gotten for the last thirty minutes anyway."

After the awkwardness of her parents' arrival, they sat and talked about the cruise while they waited for word on Maggie and the babies. A little after three-thirty, Jim emerged with a huge grin on his face. Even the fact her parents were present and hanging out with her didn't seem to faze him.

"Gabriel Aiden and Faith Ariel arrived a little after three. Maggie did great, and everyone is healthy."

Happy tears sprang to her eyes as she hurled herself at her brother-in-law for a big hug. "Awesome. When can we see them?"

He started backing up. "I'll come and get you. It will be a bit before they are finished up."

Less than an hour later, they entered Maggie's room. She lay propped up in bed and held a baby in each crook of her arms. "Mom. Dad. You're home early."

Both smiled and approached the bed. She rolled her

eyes. Obviously, her sister wasn't going to get the special stare or lecture she received. She snapped a few photos with her phone before she stepped closer. "Look how little they are." She drew a finger down the soft cheek of her new baby niece. "Beautiful."

"Do you want to hold one of them? You better do it now, because once Mom gets ahold of them, you won't get the chance."

They both laughed at their mom's affronted scowl upon her face. "I can delay my turn. But don't make me wait too long."

She settled in the nearby chair with Faith. "Hello, pretty girl. You were in a hurry to arrive, weren't you?" She glanced at Jim. "Which was born first?"

"Faith is older by about two minutes."

"Oh, so baby brother shoved you out, huh?" She held her for a bit longer before switching to hold her new nephew. He wore a scowl. "Uh oh. I've seen the same expression on your mother's face." She smiled at Maggie. "Love you, sis."

She sighed and shrugged her shoulders. "I'm too tired to reprimand you."

"Wow." She shook her head. "Someone note the date and time. This occurrence will probably never happen again."

Her mom extended her arms to take Gabriel. "Okay. I've waited patiently. Let me have one of the bundles of joy."

She sat down on the edge of the bed and viewed her parents cooing over the two newborns. "You did good, Maggie. I'm glad everyone is healthy."

Her sister touched her arm to get her attention. "Thank you for getting us here this morning, and for everything you did this week."

"You are welcome. No problem at all."

Her sister quirked a brow.

"Okay, so we had a few touch-and-go moments, but we got through it, didn't we?"

Her sister chuckled. "Some of us better than others."

As her parents switched babies with each other, she grinned. "Wow. Christmas Eve babies. What a gift."

Maggie shot her a sassy smile and winked. "I can think of another awesome gift you could have this season."

She pointed a finger at her and chuckled. "I am not sneaking Oreos into the hospital for you. I'm drawing the line."

"Not a bad idea, but I'm talking about a certain young man." She wiggled her eyebrows. "Now wouldn't he be a wonderful package to unwrap for Christmas?"

"Maggie." She gasped and stole a peek at her parents.

"What?" She exchanged an amused glance with their mom before continuing. "They know about the birds and the bees. If they'd seen the sparks flying off you two this week, they would agree with me. Especially if he can convince you to move home to Cedar Bend."

Everyone's gaze trained on her and she squirmed. "All right. All right. I won't put off talking to him about the Pilar engagement issue."

"Thank you." She glanced at their parents. "Mom. Dad. Can you pick up Taggert and bring him by to visit his new brother and sister?" She winked at Maddy. "My sister needs some alone time with her man."

Chapter Twenty-Five

Madison took a deep breath and paused on the porch. Her sister's parting words of putting her big girl panties on echoed through her mind. She's right. It was past time to screw up her courage and tell Ryder her feelings. Then she would know how to move on, with or without him.

"You okay, honey?"

She glanced at her mom. "What if he doesn't feel the same way I do?"

Her dad stepped forward and put his arm around her shoulders. "Nothing in life is guaranteed. You would kick yourself harder if you don't even try."

He was right. Now wasn't the time to hide behind her shyness and insecurities. Squaring her shoulders, she opened the door. Complete chaos met them as soon as they entered the foyer. The television played cartoon network, loudly, and as they stepped further into the house, Snow ran into the kitchen. She shook her head as she observed Taggert and Ryder on the floor constructing something from Legos.

"No, Ryder. Not like that." He sighed. "I'll show you again. Pay attention."

A giggle escaped her lips. Her nephew gave instructions to an architect on how to build something. The scene was priceless.

Hearing her laughter, Taggert jumped up and ran

over. "Is Mom okay? Are the babies here?"

Ryder rose to his feet and grabbed the remote to mute the television. He grimaced as he looked around. "Sorry about the mess."

Her dad smiled. "Looks like you could use a break."

She kneeled to peer into Taggert's eyes. "You put away your toys. Clean up your mess, and Grandma and Grandpa will take you to the hospital to meet your new sister and brother."

His eyes rounded. "Cool."

As he grabbed toys off the floor and hauled them to the nearby toy box, she shook her head. Within minutes the room was put back to rights. She glanced from beneath her lashes at Ryder. He looked a little frazzled, the poor guy. "I'm sorry we hijacked your day. It's Christmas Eve. I hope we didn't ruin any plans you may have made."

He looked at the clock on the wall. "Mom and Dad expect me for dinner in about an hour. That was the only set plans I had for the day."

A tug on her pant leg signaled her nephew's return.

"Aunt Maddy, I'm done."

Her mom held out her hand. "Come on, Tag, let's change your clothes and pack an overnight bag. You're staying at Grandma and Grandpa's tonight."

A worried frown creased his forehead. "But how will Santa find me?"

Grandma Reynolds patted his hand. "Don't worry. We are going to write him a note with directions to our house." She winked at her husband and daughter.

"Okay, Dad. There's your signal. The Santa stash is in Maggie's closet. I'll help you get the stuff in the trunk. But hurry. I don't want him catching us."

Ryder followed them down the hall. "I'll help."

She twisted around and smiled. "Thank you."

They barely made it back from outside when her nephew rushed into the living room with a clean Spiderman shirt on. "Hurry up, Grandma. You're burning daylight."

Her mom frowned as she entered the room and looked at her accusingly. "Where, I wonder, did he pick up that expression?"

She held up a hand. "Blame your oldest. I didn't do it." She crossed her heart with a finger. "Dad. Do you need help getting the car seat out of my car?"

"Don't worry, honey. We've got it. We'll see you tomorrow."

She heaved a huge sigh and plopped onto the couch as her parents left. "What a day."

He frowned and glanced at the front door. "You're not going back to the hospital with them?"

"Nope." She sighed. "I'm relieved of duty for the evening."

"Alone on Christmas Eve?" He shook his head. "Not on my watch."

Huh? She tilted her head to meet his gaze. "After the week I've had, a nice soak in the tub and some quiet sounds like heaven."

He sat down beside her on the couch. "As exciting as your plans sound, my mom would have my hide if I left you all alone tonight. Why don't you join me for dinner at my parent's house?"

Her heart hammered in her chest. "Uh. I don't think going with you to your parents is a good idea."

"Why? Because I'm engaged to Pilar?"

There it was. Out in the open. He was engaged. His words confirmed her worst fear. Pilar had told her the truth. Tears pooled in her eyes. She turned her head and stared out the window. "I'm not sure your fiancée would be keen on your invitation."

His hand cupped her cheek and drew her gaze back to his own. "I'm not, you know."

A tear escaped and traveled down her cheek. "Not what?"

He wiped away the wetness from her face. "Engaged."

It took a moment for his words to sink in. "What did you say?"

"Besides being forced to watch cartoons today, I had an interesting discussion with Taggert. For a four-year-old, he is informative." He clasped her hands in his own. His thumb softly caressed her knuckles. "It seems someone was busy getting me engaged this week…when I'm not."

"But Pilar wore your engagement ring."

He shook his head. "Correction. She borrowed her mother's wedding ring to make you think we were engaged. After Taggert asked me about marrying Pilar, I called her to confront her. She spilled her guts on the antics she played this week."

"Including the spying episode when you kissed me on the porch?" A shocked expression crossed his face. "I don't think she's told you everything." She shook her head. "I can't believe her mom let her borrow her ring."

A snort escaped his lips. "She didn't. It seems she sneaked out of the house with it and hoped to have it back before her mom missed her jewelry." He chuckled. "Things didn't go as planned when she arrived home to find her mom searching the house frantically for her ring."

"Serves her right."

His gaze didn't waver as he tapped her nose. "The thing I've been wrestling with…why did she think she had to go to so much trouble."

Confession time was upon her. Snow jumped on the couch and crawled across his knees to settle upon her lap. She looked up at her and started to purr. Absentmindedly, she started rubbing the cat under her chin. "It's probably because she knows how I feel about you."

Eagerness radiated from him as he leaned toward her. "Care to clue me in?"

She leaned her head back against the couch cushion and closed her eyes. "Do you have any idea what feelings I had for you in high school?" She opened her eyes and met his gaze. "Well, Pilar did. She realized I had the hugest crush on you. I attended all your baseball games for the chance to watch you in your tight uniform."

His lips quirked. "What about now?"

Purposely she misunderstood him. "Your butt still looks mighty fine."

He choked on a laugh. "I meant, do you still have a crush on me?"

She shook her head. "No."

Disappointment settled on his features. Could it be possible he held some affection for her after all? She leaned forward and smoothed the frown away on his forehead. "I'm not crushing on you anymore. My condition has become much worse. I'm in love with you."

A huge sigh left his body. He captured her lips in a searing kiss. Surprised by his actions, it took a moment for her to respond. Snow protested as she got squished between their bodies. He broke the kiss and placed his forehead against hers. "I'd hoped for that answer. Do you remember a school field trip we took to the botanical gardens in junior high?"

She frowned as she tried to connect his question to their discussion. What did this have to do with anything? He continued once she shook her head.

"You see, a certain freckle-faced girl shared her pudding cup with me. My mom had forgotten to pack dessert."

"Me?" She put her hands up to cover her cheeks as he nodded. "I hate my freckles sometimes."

He dragged her hands away from her face. "I don't."

She shook her head. "I'm not glamorous like Pilar."

A near choke escaped him. "Thank goodness."

"I'm quirky."

"I love your quirkiness."

Embarrassed, she refocused back on the story he'd told. "So, it is true. The way to a man's heart is through food. No matter his age."

His chest rumbled with a deep chuckle as he tucked a piece of her hair behind an ear. "I think you've won Taggert and me over with your smiley face pancakes."

"But you never asked me out."

He palmed her cheek and rubbed his thumb over her lower lip. "I tried. Daily."

"No, you did not. I would remember something like that."

"How many times did you run into me in the halls in between classes?"

She frowned as she dived deep into her memory. Scenarios from the past played through her mind. Could all those awkward meetings been his attempt to ask her out?

"I can see the wheels turning in your head. Do you remember me going out of my way to run into you? To say good morning or hello, but you always acted like I had cooties."

She rubbed her cheek against his palm. "I was so shy and had a major crush on you. You left me tongue-tied every time you spoke to me."

His lips brushed hers with a gentle kiss. "In case you haven't gathered, I'm in love with you too."

She smiled before nipping at his bottom lower lip. "You took your sweet time telling me. You could have led with I love you."

"Sorry. I guess I'm going to have to work on my timing." A crooked grin appeared on his face. "So, I no longer have cooties?"

"The verdict is still out. We will have to perform some experiments."

"Can I conduct the first one?"

"Sure."

"Can I kiss you now?"

"Permission granted." As his head descended, she held up a hand. "Wait." She rose from the couch and closed the living room curtains. "In case prying eyes have decided to spy on us this evening." She rejoined him and draped her arms around his neck. "Now. Where were we?"

His lips teased hers. "Right here." The gentle brush

disappeared as he deepened the caress.

Her breath caught as he nibbled a slow trail along her jaw and descended to nip at her neck. A soft buzzing intruded upon the moment.

The interruption made him growl. Holding up a finger, he stated, "Hold that thought." He retrieved his phone from his pocket and cleared his throat. "Hi, Mom." His smoldering gaze didn't leave hers. "Yes, I'm still coming over." He leaned in and brushed his lips against hers. "Um, Mom. Can you set another place at the table?" He smiled as he listened to his mom on the other end of the line. "It's a surprise."

She swatted his arm once he disconnected the call. "You don't surprise people with uninvited guests. Especially, on a holiday."

"Hey. I got the privilege of being intimidated by your parents today. I think turnabout is fair play."

Chapter Twenty-Six

Ryder smiled as she fidgeted in the passenger seat of his truck. They'd taken a few minutes to drop Snow off at his condo before heading to his parent's house. "Relax."

"Easy for you to say. You're not an introvert."

Her sassiness made him laugh. "Take a deep breath. We're here."

Once they reached the porch, she paused and wrung her hands. "Are you sure me being here is okay?"

Understanding her uncertainty, he grasped her hands. "Trust me. You'll be fine." He bestowed a quick kiss before he opened the door. "Mom. Dad."

A woman's voice called back, "In the living room."

After he helped her out of her coat, he shrugged out of his. Each hung in the closet before he threaded his fingers with her chilled hand and led her further into the house. "Sorry, it took so long, but I had to convince Madison I wasn't committing a social 'foo-pah' inviting her last minute to our meal." He wanted to laugh when his mom murmured to his dad, "*It's not Pilar. Thank goodness.*" Playing ignorant he asked, "Did you say something, Mom?"

"Never mind." She eased out of the recliner. "Hi, I'm Evie Sanders."

His dad extended his hand. "Max Sanders."

"Mom. Dad. This is Madison Reynolds. I don't know if you remember, but she was in my class in school. When I found out she would be alone tonight, I asked her to join us."

"I'm sorry to crash your party."

"Nonsense." Evie smiled. "It's no problem, dear. We have plenty of food."

Her nose lifted in appreciation as she sniffed the air. "It smells delicious, Mrs. Sanders."

His mom waved a hand. "Don't bother with formality. It's Evie and Max."

"You have a lovely home. The fire looks wonderful." She crossed the room to hold her hands out to the flame. "Can I help in any way with dinner?"

Ryder caught his parent's gaze and winked before he mouthed, *I'm going to marry this one*. His mom blinked at him in surprise before a smile spread across her face.

Happiness radiated from her as she patted his hand. "Max, I could use your help putting the food on the table. Can you bring in the ham, please?"

"What do you want me to do, Mom?"

Evie looked over her shoulder. "Maddy? Would you like some wine?"

She turned away from the fireplace and smiled. "Yes, please."

In the kitchen, he retrieved a bottle of wine. "Is a red okay?" He poured a glass for everyone. "Can I make a toast?" As everyone lifted their glass he continued, "To family and love, this holiday season." His gaze held hers as they clinked their glasses together. A blush rose in her cheeks, but her eyes twinkled with joy at his words.

Evie cleared her throat. "Let's sit while the food is hot. Ryder, can you say the blessing?"

As he murmured a prayer, he linked his hand with hers. Once he finished, he squeezed her hand before relinquishing it to pass her the bowl of potatoes.

Max paused with his fork midair. "So, Madison, do you still live in Cedar Bend?"

"No. I'm in Colorado Springs. I'm in town to help my sister. The doctor placed her on bed rest last week. She's pregnant with twins." She laughed and shook her head. "Well, she was. Today she delivered a healthy boy and girl."

Evie exclaimed, "How exciting. Everyone doing fine?"

She put down her spoon. "Maggie is tired, but she and the babies are well." She shifted to drag her phone from her back pocket. "Do you want to see my pictures?"

Ryder leaned over. "Hey. Not fair. You didn't show me the photos yet."

She held the phone just out of reach. "Ask nicely."

He poked her in the ribs. "You don't want to mess with this."

She giggled before offering her cell. "Okay. Okay."

He took the phone and swiped through the photos. "They sure are cute."

"Of course, they are."

He chuckled and handed the phone to his mom for her to view the pictures. "Words spoken like a proud aunt."

The nervousness Madison had displayed earlier

was gone as he observed her interacting with his mom and dad. He laughed as she retold the story of her nephew's visit to Santa a few days ago. His mind wandered from the conversation. When his dad had asked where she lived it dawned on him, they hadn't talked about the distance between where they lived and starting a new romance. He shifted nervously in his seat. Would the relationship be doomed before it began?

She noticed his restlessness and shot him a concerned peek before leaning in to whisper, "Is something wrong?"

Her unease reflected in her gaze. He shook his head and threaded his hand with hers. "We'll talk about it later." The answer didn't satisfy her, he could tell by the nervous glances she kept casting his way. "Wonderful meal, Mom. Let me help clear the dishes."

Evie smiled and leaned back in her chair. "I won't say no."

Arms stacked with a few dishes, he strode toward the kitchen.

An arm snaked around his waist. "Hey. You got so serious earlier. What's the matter?"

The plates teetered in his hands before he deposited them on the counter. With a turn, he eased her into a hug. "I'm sorry. Earlier I got caught up in the moment when we talked at Maggie's house. I have some concerns."

An expression of disbelief widened her eyes, and she started to slip out of his arms.

"Hey. Wait." He grabbed her and enfolded her back into an embrace. "My words didn't come out right. I think you misunderstood what I'm wanting to say."

The sadness still lurked in her eyes as her gaze met his. "O…kay."

A groan rose in his throat as he lifted a hand to gently brush her lips. "You live in Colorado Springs. I'm already missing you, and you haven't even left town yet."

A deep sigh of relief escaped her lips. "So, this is about logistics?"

His arms tightened around her as he nodded. "I love Cedar Bend. My business is here. I'm worried the long-distance arrangement will wear on you. I'm not sure I could handle you breaking up with me because we can't spend time together."

She rose on her tiptoes and placed her arms about his neck. "Did we, or did we not, already determine I'm not Pilar?" Her lips brushed his. "Ask me nicely."

"Hell right, you're not Pilar." The nibble at his lips distracted him for a moment. "Ask you what?"

"Where I plan to live."

His heart thumped in a wild tattoo in his chest. "Madison?"

A sweet smile appeared. "Yes, Ryder."

"Anyone ever tell you you're sassy?"

"Just Maggie."

A kernel of hope grew in his chest as he squeezed her tight. "Please don't get my hopes up, to dash them. Are you saying you'd move back to Cedar Bend?"

She bit her lip. "Only if I'm asked in a satisfying manner."

A whoop of joy escaped.

His mom and dad rushed into the kitchen. Each wore an expression of concern on their faces.

"Everything okay?"

"Who's hurt?"

He laughed as they asked simultaneous questions. "We're fine." He picked her up and swung her around.

She slugged him on the shoulder. "Hey, put me down, you big oaf. You still haven't asked."

He slid her body down the length of his until her feet were planted on the floor. "Madison Reynolds, can you please move back to Cedar Bend? To date me and be with me?"

Her eyes twinkled. "I will see what I can arrange."

"Mom. Can we have our dessert to go?"

Chapter Twenty-Seven

The dim light from the truck's dash reflected upon his face as a Christmas tune played softly in the background. Neither spoke as he extended his hand across the console to thread his fingers with hers. Awareness took hold of her body as he began to draw circles on her thumb.

Anticipation shimmied up her spine when she recognized they were driving back to his place. Not Maggie's. His continued ministrations with his thumb scattered her thoughts and goose bumps formed on her arms.

The sound of the turn signal echoed through the silence of the cab as he pulled into his drive. Moonlight reflected off the snow as he turned off the headlights. The shiver traveling down her back had nothing to do with the cold night. A gentle tug on her clasped hand brought her halfway across the console. She wasn't sure if the sigh came from her or him as he closed the distance between them.

His lips grazed hers briefly before he leaned away. "Madison. In high school, I dreamed of kissing you. It took a while, but I'm glad I finally got my wish this week."

Her arm snaked around his neck and brought his lips back to hers. The kiss turned from gentle to passionate. Both were breathless when they finally broke apart. "Much better than any schoolgirl fantasy I imagined." A giggle escaped as he dragged her across the console into his lap and accidently honked the horn. For once she wished she had her sister's shorter legs as she turned to extend her legs back into the passenger seat.

"Damn. I miss vehicles with bench seats." His growled words blurred in her mind as he slowly nibbled a trail down her neck. She shifted for him to have better access. The rasp of his five-o'clock shadow triggered an unfamiliar tingling in her limbs. With an unsteady hand, she lifted his chin. As their gazes locked, she smiled. "Best Christmas gift ever."

A dog barked nearby. "Damn." Their arms tangled as he wrestled with getting her back into the passenger seat a moment before there was a knock on the truck window.

"Mr. Sanders. Are you okay?"

Madison tried to contain her laughter as he struggled with clicking on the ignition to roll down the window.

"Good evening, Mrs. Thomas. You out for your evening stroll with Binky?"

The huskiness of his voice made the situation even funnier. Maybe she hadn't had the opportunity of getting caught necking in his vehicle in high school, but this evening made up for the lack of that experience. She covered her mouth to stifle her laughter and turned her head.

"Binky was barking her head off. We became concerned when we heard your truck horn sound. Then to see your windows all fogged over, we didn't know if you'd hit your head on the steering wheel and knocked yourself out. Binky and I were worried something bad had happened to you."

A soft groan emerged from his mouth. "I appreciate your concern, but as you can see Mrs. Thomas, I'm fine. Thank you for checking on me. I hope you and Binky have a Merry Christmas."

The older lady stood on tiptoe holding a tiny rat-looking dog and eyed her a moment before nodding. "Merry Christmas to you too, Mr. Sanders."

Both busted out with laughter as soon as the window rolled back into place. He ran a hand through his hair. "Um. Maybe we should take our party inside."

A snuffle escaped as she replied, "We don't want Binky to have a heart attack."

"Or Mrs. Thomas."

The heat of his hand on her lower back as he guided her up the walk brought back the anticipation recently interrupted. As soon as the front door clicked shut, he dipped his head to explore her lips. A moan escaped as she linked her hands behind his neck.

They broke apart and simultaneously reached for coat zippers, not breaking eye contact. She smiled when both coats fell to the floor, and in rhythm, they toed their shoes off.

"We'll worry about the mess later." His low murmur brought another smile to her lips. Entangling her hand with his, he led her to the couch nearby and pulled her down with him. A light left on in the kitchen cast a soft glow into the room.

His arms wrapped around her waist as she straddled his hips and eased down onto his lap. He gently nibbled her neck. "You smell like a summer evening."

"Mmm." It was getting harder to concentrate on his words. His lips were like lethal weapons. "Bug spray?"

His chuckle fanned her neck. "No. Like a meadow of wildflowers."

"Have you always been this good with flattery?" The question barely left her lips before he kissed her passionately. The heat engulfing her body was like flames burning through her veins. How could she get closer? Inching her hands under his sweater, she felt his stomach tighten as she dragged his top over his head. Her gaze met his for a second before she bent to trail her lips across his chest. She smiled when he inhaled a sharp breath.

On a groan he murmured, "You're overdressed."

"So I am." In an effortless lift, she removed her top.

"Much better." He leaned in to capture her lips in a brief caress before nibbling a trail down her neck.

A gasp echoed in the quiet room as he stroked her outer thighs and moved upward to release the clasp on her bra.

His eyes glowed with longing as his gaze met hers and he began to stroke her breasts.

All shyness retreated as she leaned in to nip at his earlobe. She smiled as a deep groan rattled in his chest.

Moments later, he twisted until her back met the couch cushions. A cocky grin lit his face as he rid them both of their remaining clothing. The smirk disappeared as he edged back into her embrace.

A happiness she never thought she'd experience brought tears to her eyes. "I love you, Ryder."

As he eased his body to join her own, he gave her a tender kiss. "I love you too, Madison."

Chapter Twenty-Eight

December, a year later

"It's great your sister let us use the yard ornaments you bought last year to decorate our yard."

Madison wanted to punch Santa in the nose. "Yeah, but she could have kept this big red fellow."

His deep chuckle carried across the yard. "I have a soft spot for Santa."

She twisted her head before the blow-up Santa face-planted her again. "Tell me again why I'm the only one over here battling Santa?"

He wiggled his brows. "I like the view better from over here."

She let the yard ornament fall to the ground and crossed her arms. "This elf is on strike."

"Let the negotiations begin."

She giggled as he advanced with a gleam in his eye. "Now, Mr. Sanders, don't do anything rash."

"I'm not, Mrs. Sanders."

She scooped up a handful of snow and chucked it at his chest.

He dodged the frozen missile. "Uh-oh. Seems to me like someone is definitely in trouble now."

Her smile slipped as he rushed her and gently tackled her to the ground. "Do you give?"

She caught her breath and smiled. "Nope." Seconds

later, she trickled snow down the back of his collar.

"You're making this hard for me to fight fair."

Her hands hooked behind his head. "Now you get the idea." His cool lips touched hers, and she melted.

"Mom. They're doing mushy stuff again."

She laughed as she peeked around her husband. "Hi, Taggert. Maggie."

Her sister rolled her eyes. "Newlyweds. We should have called first." She looked about. "You do realize you live on a public street, right?"

Taggert tilted his head. "Are you trying to make a snow angel? You're doing it wrong, Uncle Ryder."

He laughed, rose to his feet, and extended a hand to help her up from the ground. "I haven't had as much practice as you have, Tag."

Her nephew scanned the yard ornaments scattered about and sighed. "Aunt Maddy, did you kill Santa again?"

She held up her hands. "I'm hopeless."

Maggie shook her head. "The reason for this little impromptu visit is to invite you to dinner tonight. Jim is progressing in his cooking class and wants to show off what he has learned."

"Great." She winked at her husband. "We're past the guinea pig stage. What time?"

"Come around six. That will give you time to play with Gabe and Faith before we eat."

"It's a date." She waved to them as they backed from the drive. She was delighted to live around family again. Happiness engulfed her. So much had changed in such a short period. Her employer in Colorado Springs hadn't been happy to lose her, but she'd found a position she enjoyed at a local bank. Once the job had fallen in place, so did the rest of the logistics. Ryder bought the brick log home Alex and he had built and proposed the same day he closed on it.

A pair of strong arms embraced her from behind. "Your mind is miles away."

She rotated in his arms and snuggled against his chest. "I was reflecting on the past year." She lifted her gaze to meet his. "What would have happened if Taggert hadn't tangled us up in tinsel last year?"

His lips quirked. "I like the tangled memory better than the puking on my shoe one."

She shook her head. "You're not going to let me live down the vomiting on you, are you?"

"Not a chance." He lowered his head to claim her lips with a quick kiss. "I love you, Madison."

"Love you too, Ryder."

A word about the author...

N. Jade Gray grew up on a farm in Oklahoma with one sister and three brothers.

She began reading romance novels in high school and was hooked. In an attempt to entertain her friends, she began writing stories. The biggest hurdle she had to overcome with her writing was sharing her stories. Her former writing groups, the Wichita and Regional Authors and Low Country Romance Writers, helped with her confidence and shook the needed pom-poms to get her motivated for publication. She is also a former member of the Romance Writers of America.

She met her husband while attending college and has two grown sons. Not really knowing what she wanted to do when she grew up, she's held various jobs in the accounting and legal fields. She lives in Kansas with her husband, rescue cats Meera, Mango, and Pancake, and one spoiled dog named Fabio. Yes, she helped named the dog. She loves to hear her husband calling for his four-legged companion.

Visit the author at:

www.njadegray.com

Thank you for purchasing
this publication of The Wild Rose Press, Inc.

For questions or more information
contact us at
info@thewildrosepress.com.

The Wild Rose Press, Inc.
www.thewildrosepress.com